CRITICAL ERROR

TRIUMPH OVER ADVERSITY

LYNN SHANNON

CT
Creative Thoughts

CRITICAL ERROR

This novel is dedicated to the families of our brave soldiers. Thank you for all that you do.

And God is able to bless you abundantly, so that in all things at all times, having all that you need, you will abound in every good work.

2 Corinthians 9:8

ONE

"We have a problem."

Cassie Miles tossed a glance toward the barn door. Papa Joe was moving in her direction, his long stride hampered by the orthopedic boot clasped on his right foot. A crumpled cowboy hat hid his thinning gray hair and shadowed his eyes. Cassie tightened her grip on the mane comb. Her horse, Starlight, nickered softly as if picking up on her tension.

What now? Cassie was tempted to duck back inside the stall and ignore whatever new problem had arisen. She was drowning in trouble as it was. Bank account running close to empty? Check. Delays in construction of her nonprofit horse rehabilitation center? Check. An aging grandfather with a heart condition who refused to give up fried foods? Check. Add in the creepy texts and phone calls she'd been receiving lately...

A shudder rippled down her spine. She'd changed her phone number twice, but her stalker uncovered it each time. Cassie had reported the communications to the Knoxville Police Department, but there wasn't much anyone could do. Whoever was sending the messages used different burner phones. She kept telling herself it was nothing, but things were getting increasingly scary. The texts included details about the clothes she wore, her hairstyles, and the errands she'd been on.

Sugar plum. That's what he called her in every text. Cassie had passed plums in the grocery store last week and nearly thrown up right there in the produce section. She'd never be able to see the fruit again without fear twisting her insides.

Cassie loosened her grip on the mane comb. Her fingers ached from holding it so tightly. She focused on her grandfather. "What's wrong, Papa Joe?"

He frowned, the wrinkles along the corners of his mouth deepening. "It's Eric."

Eric Leighton. Twenty years old and autistic, he was the closest thing Cassie had to a little brother. They'd grown up together on Papa Joe's small ranch. Eric and his mother, Bessie, lived in a house on the far end of the property. She'd arrived in Knoxville as a single mother, desperate for a job and little money to her name. Papa Joe had taken Bessie and Eric in. Just like he'd done with Cassie one year later.

She'd arrived at her paternal grandfather's house as troublesome twelve-year-old with a chip the size of Texas on her shoulder. Papa Joe's patience and steadiness had softened the rough edges caused by an early childhood full of neglect. He was the best man she'd ever known.

Papa Joe, Bessie, and Eric. They were her family.

"Bessie called," Papa Joe continued. "Eric isn't home yet."

Concern rippled through Cassie. Dusk was approaching fast, and Eric feared the dark. The route to his house was a ten-minute horse ride. "Eric left over thirty minutes ago. He should've arrived home by now."

"Bessie drove the route to the river but didn't see him. The banks are overflowing from all the rain we've had the last few days. She thinks Eric got confused about where the bridge is and lost his way."

It was possible. Eric consistently used the same route from his house to Papa Joe's place, and vice versa. Any disparity, like a fallen log along the path, or in this case, the overflowing river banks, upset him. Cassidy set the mane comb down on a ledge. "I'll ride out and find him. Can you call Bessie to let her know?"

He headed for the barn office while Cassie darted into the tack room. She snagged Starlight's saddle, and within three minutes, the white gelding was ready to go. Cassie mounted her horse just as Papa Joe came hobbling out of the office. "Wait."

He carried a handgun in one hand, along with a holster. Papa Joe offered the items to Cassie. "Take this with you."

"I don't need that." Cassie knew how to shoot, thanks to Papa Joe's training, but she wasn't particularly fond of guns.

"There have been some strange things happening on the property lately, not to mention those creepy texts you've been getting. Take it just in case." Papa Joe met her gaze. "It'll make this old man feel better."

Her stalker couldn't have anything to do with Eric's disappearance. There *had* been several mishaps on the property, but they were most likely attributed to the construction crews coming and going. Cassie wrestled with the urge to argue with Papa Joe, but it would waste time. And she wouldn't purposefully worry her grandfather.

With a sigh, she accepted the gun. Cassie made sure the weapon was loaded and the safety was on. Then she secured the holster in the small of her back before tugging her shirt over it. "I have my cell. Call if Eric makes it home before I find him."

"Will do."

She clicked her tongue and tapped Starlight's flank with her heels. The horse obediently moved forward, and moments later, they were flying across the pasture. Warm spring wind rippled Cassie's ponytail. Dandelions poked through the tender blades of grass and the woods near the river were flush with foliage. She knew every inch of this land. Had spent thousands of hours learning its secrets as a child. For the last eight years, she'd been living in North Carolina—first for college and then for work. Moving home had been a good decision.

Cassie slowed Starlight as they neared the woods. The trail leading to the bridge was wide enough for a vehicle. It was cleared regularly of debris and the trees were trimmed. Eric wasn't the only one who used this path. They all did.

"Eric! It's Cassie. Can you hear me?"

The rushing sound of the river dividing the property swallowed her words. Cassie swung her gaze left and right, searching for any sign of her surrogate little brother.

Nothing.

She kept calling. The sun was setting fast, leaching color from the sky. It worried her. These woods became pitch-black at night, something that would terrify Eric. His horse, a gentle palomino named Casper, was well-trained, and Eric was an excellent rider. Still, he could've been hurt...

Papa Joe's concerns about her stalker flared in Cassie's mind. Goose bumps broke out across her skin and the weight of the gun settled in the small of her back became heavier. She shook off the nerves. Entertaining wild theories wouldn't help. Neither would freaking herself out.

At a fork in the trail, a flash of color caught her eye. There. Eric had been wearing a red shirt today. He must've gone left inside of right. Probably gotten himself turned around. Cassie steered Starlight toward the small cemetery. It was family only, generations of Miles, all in the same place. Her father and grandmother were buried here. They'd both died before she'd arrived to live with Papa Joe. Her father in a car accident before she was born, her grandmother of cancer.

Casper, Eric's horse, came into view. He was standing under the branches of a giant oak tree and nickered at the sight of Starlight. Cassie's breath hitched. Eric lay crying in a fetal position a short distance away, near a weathered tombstone. His red shirt and blue jeans were a sharp contrast to the green grass. She dismounted and raced to his side. What had happened? Had she been wrong about Casper? Had the horse been spooked by something—a snake perhaps —and thrown Eric?

Dropping to her knees, Cassie gently touched his shoulder. Blood speckled his neck. More was in his hair. "Eric, what happened?"

He didn't answer. His eyes were clamped shut, tears flowing down his face. Cassie's heart broke. She continued to speak to him in soothing words while fumbling for the cell phone in her pocket.

Wind whispered across her ponytail, raising the hair on the back of her neck. Cassie spun.

A man in dark clothes and a ski mask rushed her. Cassie half rose, instinctively protecting Eric still lying on the ground. The attacker slammed into her with the force of a linebacker. She collided with a tombstone. Her head rapped against the unyielding concrete and stars exploded across her vision. The pain stole her breath.

Cassie blinked to clear her vision. The holstered handgun pressed against the small of her back. She reached for the weapon, but her attacker was on her in an instant. She attempted to fight him, frantic movements born of panic and instinct, but her petite form was no match for his brute strength.

He secured her wrists behind her back. Then he yanked Cassie to her feet, pressing her against the ancient oak tree. Bark tangled with her hair. Bile rose in the back of her throat as the weight of his body pushed against her. The ski mask hid his features. Even his eyes were dark recesses of evil that sent terror shooting through her veins. She screamed.

He clamped a gloved hand over her mouth, silencing her cry. His fingers dug into the delicate skin on her cheek as he forced Cassie to turn her head. She stiffened as he leaned closer to her throat and inhaled deeply. Her heart thundered against her rib cage. Tears, unbidden, sprang to her eyes.

"At last, sugar plum." His breath whispered over her skin. "You're mine."

TWO

Was this a horrible idea?

Nathan Hollister touched the handmade wooden sign on the gate. The words River Ranch Horse Rescue had been burned into the hunk of pine. He trailed his fingers over the letters, a mix of emotions threading through him. Cassie had always talked about opening her own horse rehabilitation center. She'd followed through on her dream.

Cassie. His ex-fiancée. They'd grown up in the same town, but the difference in their ages meant they hadn't known each other. It'd taken a flat tire in South Carolina for them to meet. He'd been stationed at the army base. She'd been studying for her undergrad. Fate, so he'd thought at the time, had brought them together. Until Nathan destroyed the love they'd so carefully built with a decision he couldn't undo.

He continued down the dirt road. Gold and muted pinks streaked the sky as dusk transitioned to twilight. Flowers danced in the breeze along the walkway leading to the front porch. The farmhouse hadn't changed in the four years since he'd seen it. Even the shutter on the left window was still crooked. Nathan knocked on the bright red door, nerves jittering his inside.

No one answered.

He knocked again. There was no movement inside the house. His gaze swept across the property, landing on the barn. The main door was open, light spilling across the grass. Again, indecision warred within him. Nathan didn't want to hurt Cassie or cause her more pain than he already had. His presence at her home would be unwelcome. But his choices were limited. Deal with it now, in private, or risk a public encounter.

Nathan ignored the rumor mill, but rumblings still reached his ears from time to time. Cassie had moved back to her grandfather's ranch several months ago. Knoxville, Texas was a small town. Nathan and Cassie would run into each other eventually. It would be far better for their rocky reunion to happen beyond the eyes and ears of busybodies. He needed to do this.

The path through the grass leading to the barn was well worn. Last night's thunderstorms had left the ground damp, despite the day of sunshine. Nathan stepped into the barn. The unmistakable sound of a shotgun being pumped made him freeze in place.

"Hands in the air," a gravelly voice ordered from behind.

The heavy Texas accent and sharp tone were unmistakable. Joe Miles, aka Papa Joe. Nathan complied with the order. For half a heartbeat, he wondered if Cassie's grandfather intended to shoot him. Papa Joe wasn't a violent man, by any means, but Nathan hadn't treated his granddaughter right. He wouldn't blame the older man for the temptation.

"Identify yourself," Papa Joe said.

Confusion ricocheted through Nathan. It wasn't normal to greet visitors to the ranch with the dangerous end of a shotgun. Especially for Papa Joe. Something wasn't right. "It's Nathan Hollister, sir."

He felt, rather than saw, Papa Joe lower the weapon. Nathan turned on his heel to face the older man. Dark eyes raked over his face as momentary shock melted away. It was replaced with a dark cloud of anger.

Papa Joe's grip on the shotgun tightened. "What are you doing sneaking around my property?"

The question heightened Nathan's concern. "I wasn't sneaking around. I knocked on the front door and, when no one answered, saw the barn was open and thought someone might be inside."

"I didn't hear your vehicle."

"I parked at the main gate. It was locked, but the walk-though gate was open." He rocked back on his heels. It was wiser to keep his nose out of Papa Joe's business, especially given the circumstances, but Nathan had never been very good at ignoring what was right in front of his face. "Do you always carry around a shotgun to greet guests these days?"

Papa Joe grunted. He leaned the weapon against the wall of the barn. "We've been having some trouble lately."

"What kind of trouble?"

"Ain't none of your concern." The older man jutted his chin up, pegging Nathan with a hard look. "What are you doing here, anyway?"

He resisted the urge to shift his feet under Papa Joe's stare. Heat crept up his neck. Nathan hadn't only destroyed his relationship with Cassie when he'd left her at the altar. He'd ruined Papa Joe's trust in him as well. "I came to see Cassie."

"About four years too late, wouldn't you say?"

"It's long overdue. I'll give you that—"

Papa Joe raised his hand, cutting Nathan off. "Save your excuses and apologies for Cassie. Although I doubt she'll listen to 'em. She ain't here at the moment. You'll have to wait."

Nathan gestured to the walking boot on Papa Joe's right leg. "What happened to your foot?"

"The contractor building our new barn startled a mare. She stomped on my foot and—"

Gunshots erupted. Nathan's heart rate jumped. The sound wasn't uncommon in the countryside, but coupled with Papa Joe's strange behavior, it put Nathan on edge. His attention went to the yard beyond the barn doors. "What was that?"

Papa Joe paled. "Cassie. She's in trouble."

The words seized Nathan's chest and stole his breath. A thousand questions burning his tongue, but he shoved them all aside except for one. "Where is she?"

"Down by the river, on the trail." Papa Joe tossed Nathan a set of keys before snagging the shotgun. The older man hurried as fast as his limped gate would allow toward a dust-covered truck parked next to the barn. "You drive."

Nathan raced to the driver's side door and cranked the engine just as Papa Joe hauled himself into the passenger seat. The moment his door was closed, Nathan slammed on the gas. The truck was old, but responsive. Hay bales in the bed bounced as they flew over the pasture to the tree line. Papa Joe quickly explained about Eric getting lost and Cassie going to find him.

The forest embraced them. Nathan didn't slow down as he steered toward the river. His only thought was getting to Cassie. Nothing else mattered.

Please, Lord, don't let me be too late.

Papa Joe's arm shot out as they approached a fork in the road. "Cemetery. I see horses."

Nathan gripped the steering wheel as he took the turn. Moments later, the ancient oak tree standing sentry over the tombstones came into view. Two horses grazed nearby. A man—Eric—lay on the ground. Nathan's gaze swept the area, his special forces training kicking into high gear. No sign of Cassie.

He stomped on the brakes and ejected from the vehicle. Nathan yanked his concealed handgun from its holster at the small of his back. Three strides brought him to Eric's side. Blood coated the young man's head. His eyes were open but unfocused. Tear tracks mixed with dirt on his face.

Nathan's heart clenched tight. He didn't know what happened to Eric, but judging from his condition, it wasn't good.

In the grass nearby lay a discarded handgun. Cassie's? Had to be. There were signs of a struggle. Blood on a tombstone. Crushed grass. The broken zip tie lying near the handgun sent a wave of fresh adrenaline through Nathan's veins. He crouched next to Eric. "Where's Cassie?"

Eric didn't move. Papa Joe's labored breathing came up behind Nathan. "Eric, please. Where's Cassie?"

The young man didn't answer. He lifted one shaking hand, pointing toward the ridge of trees along the river bank.

Nathan bolted. His cowboy boots slipped in the grass. Tree branches tugged at his clothes, scraping the skin on his neck. The roar of the river grew louder, mingled with something else. The sound of an engine.

A boat. In quick snaps, Nathan assessed the situation. Cassie, her blond hair and petite form unmistakable even in the twilight, wrestled with a masked man on a small fishing boat thirty yards away. Her hands were tied behind her back.

The attacker's head swiveled as he caught sight of Nathan emerging from the trees. Nathan raised his gun, but didn't have a clear shot. Not without running the risk of hitting Cassie. He powered more fuel into his legs, aiming to close the distance between them. Tree roots threatened to upend him. His boots flung water with every step. The river, swollen by the recent rain water, rushed and tumbled around rocks at the edge.

The attacker shoved Cassie down in the boat and yanked the rope mooring his boat to a bolder. The fishing vessel flew into the water. Nathan raised his gun, held his breath, and fired. The shot struck the side of the boat. The speed of the vessel and the encroaching darkness impeded his visibility.

Panic threatened to overwhelm him, but years of military training kept it at bay. He put his attention to racing along the shoreline. Closing the distance would give him a better shot. He needed one. Only one.

Cassie stood up. With horror, Nathan realized her intention a second before she threw herself over the side of the boat and into the rushing water. It was a desperate move to save herself from the attacker. But with her hands tied, there was no way she could swim. She'd drown.

Nathan slid to a halt and tore his boots off. The current would bring her downstream, in his direction. But every second counted. Even if he found Cassie in the darkness, the raging river was dangerous. It could kill them both.

He dove into the frigid water.

THREE

Two hours later, Cassie held a bag of peas against the goose egg on the side of her head. The scent of fresh coffee fragranced the kitchen air. A mug sat in front of her, untouched, on the oak table. She couldn't bear to think of putting anything in her stomach.

Finally, sugar plum. You're mine.

The whispered words echoed in her mind like a horror movie she couldn't forget. She had a stalker. One willing to hurt others—like Eric—to capture her. It was terrifying. And if that wasn't enough, Cassie had been rescued by the one man she'd hoped never to see again.

Nathan Hollister.

He leaned against the island, muscular arms crossed over his broad chest. Four years had done nothing to dispel his incredible good looks. His sable brown hair was chopped short in military fashion—high and tight. It suited the angles of his face. Sharp cheek-bones, an arresting mouth, and a deep cleft in his chin.

Their eyes met across the room. Cassie's heart thumped once. Twice. The memory of Nathan's tender embrace as he pulled her from the raging river flashed in her mind. An unwanted and unexpected heat crept into her cheeks.

She tore her gaze from his. Self-recrimination followed. Being attracted to Nathan was out of the question. The man had, quite literally, left her at the altar.

A new memory washed through her. Standing in the church annex, listening to the rustle of her wedding dress as the bridesmaids arranged the fabric, as nervous anticipation twisted her insides. Kyle, Nathan's cousin and best man, strolled toward her. Cassie had known the moment she saw his face that something was wrong.

Kyle didn't say a word. He'd simply handed her a note from Nathan with two sentences scrawled in his block lettering.

I can't do this. I'm sorry.

It was the last communication she'd had with Nathan...until now.

"You mentioned the assailant was wearing a ski mask over his face." Chief of Police Sam Garcia said, drawing Cassie's attention to him. He was seated across the table from her, pen poised above his small pad. "But was anything about him familiar to you? His voice? The shape of his body?"

Cassie shook her head, stopping immediately as shooting pain ripped down her neck. She was going to be hurting tomorrow. "No. I didn't even get a good look at his eyes. Eric may have seen more."

Anger pulsed through Cassie. Forget what happened to her. She wanted to rip the criminal to shreds for what he'd done to Eric. He'd been terrorized and hurt. Fortunately, he'd walked away from the encounter with a minor bump to the head, but it would take a long time for him to recover from the trauma. If ever.

Chief Garcia sighed. He'd worked for the Knoxville Police Department since she was a teenager but had only taken over as chief last year. A scandal of some sort had forced the previous chief into retirement after months of battling with the city council. Cassie knew little about it since she hadn't been living in Knoxville at the time.

The chief's dark hair was more gray than brown and the lines bracketing his mouth had grown deeper over the years. Tonight, he looked weary. "I attempted to interview Eric this evening, but he was too shaken up to answer my questions. I'll talk to him again tomorrow. When was the last time you received a text message or phone call from the stalker?"

"Yesterday. I went to the pharmacy for Papa Joe's medication refill, and he called an hour later." A shudder ran down her spine that had nothing to do with the cold bag of peas pressed against her scalp. "He complimented me on my blouse before hanging up."

"If you heard his voice again, would you recognize it?"

"No. He uses something to disguise his voice."

"And these issues on the ranch..." He glanced down at his notebook. "The moved lawn chairs, the broken lock on the gate, and the disturbed flower pots near the back door. These things happened after you started receiving the phone calls and the texts?"

"Yes." Papa Joe glowered. "I think someone has been sneaking around the property at night."

She lowered the bag of peas from her head. "Or those things could be unrelated. There've been construction workers on the property in the last few months since we're building a new barn. Any of them could've messed with the gate or moved the lawn chairs."

"It's unlikely." Nathan's voice was low but commanding. "The barn is yards away from the house. There's no reason for a construction worker to move potted plants away from a window."

"As much as I hate to say it, Nathan has a point." Chief Garcia shot Cassie a sympathetic look before snapping his pen closed. "You need to use extra caution from here on out. Try not to go anywhere alone. In the meantime, I'll tell my officers to make extra patrols near the ranch. We're a small staff, but we want the townsfolk to feel safe. I'm sorry this happened, Cassie, and I won't stop until we find the culprit responsible."

"Thank you, Chief." She knew he would do his best, but would it be enough? Knoxville Police Department only had five full-time police officers, and they had an entire town to look after. No one could keep guard over the property 24-7.

The enormity of the evening and the threat against her settled on Cassie's shoulders like a wet horse blanket. Papa Joe rose from his chair and followed Chief Garcia onto the porch. Their voices faded behind the slap of the screen door.

Nathan jerked his chin toward the peas resting on the table. "Put more ice on your head." His gaze swept over her face, lingering on the goose end barely hidden in her hair. "Better yet, let me drive you to the hospital and have a doctor exam you."

His tone sliced through the last of Cassie's self-control. Normally, it was difficult to get a rise out of her, but tonight had used the last reserves of her patience. Her temper flared. "I don't need you to tell me what to do, Nathan. Never did, in case you hadn't noticed."

She rose from the chair and marched across the kitchen. Her stupid head was pounding, but she wouldn't give Nathan the satisfaction of being right. Childish, yes. But Cassie couldn't stop herself from opening the freezer and shoving the peas back inside. She spun on her heel to face him. "What are you doing here?"

He pressed his palms against the island. "I'm living in Knoxville, with my aunt and uncle again. I thought we might run into each other and it'd be best if it didn't happen in the feed store."

Could this night get any worse? Having Nathan standing in her kitchen was awful enough. Knowing that he was living less than twenty miles away...accidentally bumping into him in town...it was enough to ratchet up her anxiety.

Cassie didn't let any of the worries flitting through her mind show on her face. She'd mastered hiding her true self away decades ago, as a child. A self-defense mechanism born out of survival. As far as Nathan was concerned, he meant nothing to her. He *should* mean nothing to her.

She squared her shoulders. "Thanks for letting me know, but our breakup was a long time ago. We're strangers to each other now. In fact, I don't think we ever really knew each other at all."

He winced as that barb landed. Cassie refused to stop. "There's no need to say anything if we see each other in town. Pretend I don't exist. I prefer it."

He met her gaze. "I can't do that, Cassie. You're in danger. I can help. Tonight—"

"Tonight doesn't change a thing." Her tone came out sharper than she intended. Cassie sucked in a breath. "Thank you for what you did today, but I don't need or want your help. Ever. There's nothing left to say."

Hot tears pressed against the back of her eyes. She had to get out of here. Away from him, before the last shred of pride she had spilled all over the tile floor. Cassie pulled open the back door, the wash of spring air cooling her overheated cheeks. "I trust you can show yourself out."

The screen door slammed behind her. Cassie hurried down the porch, past Papa Joe in his rocking chair, and headed for the barn. A desire to pray welled up inside her, but she quashed it. She and God hadn't spoken in a very long time.

Like her mother and Nathan, He'd abandoned her too.

FOUR

That...could have gone better.

Nathan stood in the kitchen, heart in his throat, and watched Cassie march across the yard to the barn. Her shoulders were ramrod straight, her hair—the color of golden sunshine—bounced with the force of each determined step. She'd always been a force of nature. Strong-willed, tenacious, and stubbornly set on taking care of herself.

This time, it could get her killed. She was in danger. From who wasn't certain, but based on the information Cassie provided the police, she had a stalker. The criminal had nearly kidnapped her today.

Nathan had been to war and back. Been shot, more than once. Nearly died. But those moments in the river searching for Cassie were some of the most terrifying of his life. What was he supposed to do now? Walk away and pray Chief Garcia caught Cassie's stalker before he could strike again?

Impossible. But equally unrealistic was Cassie agreeing to accept his protection. She hated him. With good reason. And Nathan seriously doubted she'd accept help from anyone he knew, either. Trust had never come easily to Cassie. She had good reasons for that too.

He should've talked to her. Anything would've been better than ordering her to put ice on her head. Nathan had practiced his speech a thousand times, run it through his head over and over, but one look at those flashing brown eyes and he was lost. All his excuses and reasons for leaving on their wedding day melted away like butter left in the scorching sun. He was a fool. Nothing he could say would ever heal the wound he'd inflicted on her heart.

Nathan stepped onto the porch. Stars painted the night with all their glory, and a full moon hung low in the sky. Cicadas sang. He took a deep breath of grass-scented air and let it out slowly. It didn't ease the tension in his muscles. He'd come here on a mission to apologize to Cassie and somehow made everything worse.

Gus, Papa Joe's coonhound, rose from his place on the porch. His muzzle was mostly gray and his eyes cloudy with cataracts. Nathan scratched the dog behind his ears. "Hey, there, old boy."

The rhythmic creaking of Papa Joe's rocking chair stopped. "You did a good thing today, Nathan, and I'm grateful. But what happened in that kitchen just now..." He shook his head. "That was the best you could do?"

"No, sir." Nathan sighed. "Not even close."

Papa Joe grunted. "I thought as much. So what's the plan, soldier?"

"Convince her to accept my help."

There was no other option. Nathan patted Gus one more time and then rose. He started to take a step forward, but the butt of Papa Joe's shotgun jutted out, halting his forward momentum.

The old man's eyes narrowed. "Cassie needs your protection. There's no doubt about that. But don't you dare go into that barn unless you're ready to tell her the truth. All of it. Understand?"

"Yes, sir."

Papa Joe held his gaze and then nodded. He pulled his shotgun out of the way. Nathan stepped off the porch, ignoring the ache in his leg. He'd been shot stateside last year while helping his friend Jason.

The wound had healed, but rescuing Cassie from her attacker had tested the boundaries of his recovery.

Nathan eased the weathered barn door open. The scent of horses and hay mingled with saddle oil. The floor was dirt, and the ceiling had exposed wooden beams. It was dim inside, the only light filtering into the main walkway from the open office door.

Cassie stood next to a stall, stroking a white horse. Tears tracks carved a path down the delicate curve of her cheeks. The sight of them punched Nathan in the gut, knocking the wind from him. He wanted to close the distance between them, gather Cassie in his arms, and comfort her. But he couldn't. She would never allow it. And the pain of that fact clawed his insides with shame and regret. His fingers brushed against the cross and dog tags hidden beneath his shirt.

God, please help me find the right words here.

Starlight—based on the name written at the top of the stall door—caught Nathan's scent. The horse's nostrils flared. Cassie's head turned, and Nathan knew she'd caught sight of him when her shoulders stiffened. She swiped at the wetness on her face. Heat colored her cheeks and her mouth opened, presumably to tell him off.

"I almost died in Afghanistan," Nathan blurted out.

Cassie's brow furrowed and her mouth snapped shut. Not the most elegant way to start the conversation, but Nathan didn't have the luxury of tiptoeing around things anymore. He needed to say this.

"It was during a rescue mission. The hostage was a doctor. American. He worked for a nonprofit that trained Afghan doctors, and while returning from a small rural hospital, he was captured by terrorists. Initially, the extraction went as planned." Nathan's heart picked up speed as memories assaulted his senses. The glow of night vision goggles, the feel of his weapon in his hands, the desert sand coating his uniform and any exposed skin. "We disarmed the guards and located the doctor easily. But as I was escorting him out of enemy camp, several more terrorists ambushed us."

Nathan had shoved the doctor behind him, as was his duty and his responsibility. Even knowing what he did now, he would make the same choice. The decision had saved the man's life. "Three bullets cut right through my body armor. One came perilously close to nicking my heart. My team rescued me and the doctor, but I coded several times before reaching the hospital."

Cassie's eyes widened slightly, but she didn't speak. He paused. Nathan had never told anyone this next part. It required baring his soul, but he wouldn't do this halfway. Cassie deserved better. She always had.

"Some people say their life flashes before their eyes." Nathan breathed out. "Not me. As I fell to the ground, before losing consciousness, it was your face I saw. The biggest regret of my life was walking away from you, Cassie, and I'm sorry for the pain I caused you."

A sudden lump formed in his throat and he swallowed it down. Shame whirled inside him. Leaving her wasn't just his biggest regret; it was the worst thing he ever could've done to her. Cassie's mother had abandoned her when she was twelve. Sent her inside the grocery store for a candy bar and then drove away. It was a deep wound, which Nathan had known about.

And then he essentially did the same thing.

He'd done it to protect her, but that didn't matter. The end result was the same. And he wouldn't blame Cassie one bit if she never forgave him. "That's what I really came to tell you tonight."

She stared at a spot on the floor, her expression painfully blank. Cassie had always been hard to read, but now...it felt like a valley stood between them. Nathan had no idea what she was thinking.

Finally, she lifted her gaze to meet his. There was no emotion in her gorgeous brown eyes. It was as if she'd placed a protective shield in front of her emotions. Nathan didn't blame her one bit for that either. But it killed him all the same.

She licked her lips. "I don't know what to say."

"There's nothing for you to say. The damage is done. I know

there's no chance of us ever getting back together. But you're in trouble, Cassie, and I have the skills to keep you safe. Let me."

She didn't answer, but Nathan sensed some of her initial resistance waning. Cassie absently stroked the bridge of Starlight's nose. She wasn't foolish. She was wise enough to have deduced tonight's attack had been well-planned. Failing would only anger her stalker. There was no doubt he'd try for Cassie again.

Nathan stepped closer until he was standing in front of her. "If you don't accept for yourself, then do it for Papa Joe. For Eric and Bessie. It would break their hearts if something happened to you."

She glared at him. "That's a cheap shot, Hollister."

"It's also the truth."

Cassie dropped her hand from Starlight's muzzle. She turned away from Nathan, taking several steps toward the office. It was a tactic he knew well from their time together. When faced with a difficult conversation, or a choice she didn't like, Cassie's instinct was to bail. But there was no escaping a stalker.

Her fingers balled into fists and the line of her shoulders was tense. She seemed to wrestle with her decision.

Nathan held his breath and waited.

FIVE

Why had she said yes to Nathan?

Cassie poured a cup of coffee into a mug and rolled her tight shoulders. She usually loved mornings. Each one brought a sense of renewal, a clean slate to work from. Not today. Sleep had been elusive last night, and when it finally claimed her, she had nightmares. She was exhausted and grumpy.

It hadn't helped matters knowing Nathan was in the guest bedroom. He'd run home last night, packed a bag, and returned. Cassie went back and forth with her decision to accept his help half a dozen times. But no matter how she turned it, there was no easy solution. Last night's attack had shaken her to the core. She'd been strong enough to refuse Nathan's protection once, but not a second time.

As for his regrets about walking away on their wedding day...she hadn't sorted out her feelings on that subject.

Papa Joe was seated at the kitchen table, reading the newspaper. Cassie refilled the mug at his elbow and eyed his mostly empty breakfast plate. "That doesn't look like the turkey bacon I bought for you last week."

"Because it ain't."

She gripped her mug tighter. "The doctor specifically said—"

"Cassie, I'm eighty years old." He scowled. "If I want to eat real bacon, then I'm going to. I don't need you or Doctor Wallaby to tell me different. I've got one foot in the grave as it is."

"Don't talk like that." She couldn't bear to think of losing her grandfather. She knew he wouldn't live forever, but there was no need to hasten the process.

Cassie debated continuing the conversation, but this wasn't an argument she'd win today. Nor did she have the energy for it. She took a long sip of her coffee, glancing at the clock on the microwave. "It's late. I'd better take care of the horses."

"Already done. Nathan was up bright and early this morning. He's in the barn. You should take him a cup of coffee though. He hasn't had any yet."

Papa Joe's expression was innocent enough, but she caught the faint whiff of matchmaking in his tone. He'd always like Nathan. Yesterday's dramatic rescue seemed to have reignited those feelings in spite of the left-at-the-altar debacle. Cassie squinted. "Nathan is only here until Chief Garcia catches the lunatic stalking me."

"Yep. And while he's here, you should be polite." Papa Joe's newspaper rustled as he turned the page. "Take the man some coffee."

Cassie sighed. As much as she hated to admit it, Papa Joe was right. Nathan wasn't going anywhere for the time being. There was no need to make this harder than it needed to be.

Coffee in hand, she stepped outside. Dark clouds hovered in the distance, matching her mood. The air smelled of grass and pine. A butterfly fluttered near the open barn doors. In the fenced pasture, the horses grazed.

Nathan was spreading fresh hay in Starlight's stall. Pieces clung to his gray T-shirt, drawing attention to the rippling muscles in his arms. He wore low-slung jeans and cowboy boots, but had forgone the normal Stetson for a fraying ball cap.

Cassie's mouth went dry. She'd forgotten. Last night, her attraction to Nathan had been tempered by the stalker's attack. This morning, there was no escaping the sudden rush of awareness slamming into her with the force of a runaway stallion. Again, she second-guessed the wisdom of accepting his protection. But what other choice did she have?

Her footsteps had been silent, but somehow, Nathan still sensed her presence. He glanced up and their eyes met. Just like last night, Cassie's traitorous heart picked up speed. Nathan's easy smile didn't help matters. The dimple in his left cheek winked. She gripped the coffee mugs so tightly it was any wonder they didn't shatter in her hands.

"Morning." He exited the stall, pulling off his work gloves and tucking them into the back pocket of his faded jeans. The movement shifted his shirtsleeve. A scar peeked out, the mottled skin raised and slightly red. A bullet wound? Judging from the shape, it appeared so. Nathan had mentioned being shot three times. Almost dying.

The physical sight of his scar made their conversation last night all too real. A tangle of emotions washed through Cassie. She was angry and hurt, but the thought of Nathan dying left a sour taste in her mouth. That coupled with his bravery last night...it made for a confusing mess.

"Here." She shoved one of the coffee mugs in his direction. The liquid sloshed over the rim and Cassie winced as it scalded her hand. She mentally berated herself for being so foolish.

Nathan took the offered mug. "Did you burn yourself?"

He tried to capture her hand to see for himself, but Cassie yanked it back. She swiped her thumb against the back of her jeans. The skin was a touch red, but it would pass. "I'm fine."

An awkward silence descended between them. Cassie sipped her coffee and then cleared her throat. "Thank you for taking care of the horses."

His mouth twitched, amusement flickering in his eyes. "You

25

nearly choked on those words. Out of practice saying thank you? Or is it only me?"

She laughed, and some of her uneasiness softened. "A bit of both. I'm used to doing most things on my own, although Eric comes and helps a lot."

"How is he? Have you spoken to him this morning?"

"He's doing much better. Bessie is going to bring him by later to see the horses." She strolled to the opposite side of the barn. The door opened to the gated pasture, and a breeze ruffled her hair. Cassie had tried to pull it into a ponytail this morning, but the goose egg from last night ached too much. She tucked a strand behind her ear. "Any of the horses give you trouble?"

"The palomino is a bit skittish, but nothing I couldn't handle."

"She's a rescue. I've only had her a few weeks." She gestured to the new barn, several yards away. It was painted a pretty red with white trim. "There are a few small things to finish on the new barn. Then I'll be able to house up to ten horses. My nonprofit is the only one of its kind in this area. We'll be servicing over thirty counties."

"That's amazing. I'm proud of you, Cassie."

His words sent warmth spreading through her insides. She tamped it down. It shouldn't matter what Nathan thought of her. What she'd told Papa Joe earlier was true. Nathan was only here until the man stalking her was arrested. Then they would go their separate ways.

She shrugged. "Rescuing horses doesn't pay the bills. I work at the animal shelter in town. In fact, I have to be at work soon." She eyed him. "I suppose you'll be coming with me."

"Yep." Nathan drained the last of his coffee. "But before we go, I have some questions about your stalker, Cassie."

"What kind of questions? You were there for my conversation with Chief Garcia. I told him everything I knew."

"Yes, but I don't believe this guy is a stranger. He disguises his voice on phone calls with you because he's afraid you'll recognize him."

An icy finger of dread touched the back of her neck. "I can't think of anyone who would stalk me."

Nathan's gaze skittered away from hers. His fingers turned white as he gripped the coffee mug. "What about a former boyfriend?"

Cassie's cheeks heated. She wanted the earth to swallow her up right there. The horrifying truth was that she hadn't had a steady boyfriend since their breakup. It was something she really didn't want to admit to Nathan. Nor did she like the twisty way her mind immediately imagined all the women he must've dated in the last four years.

She ran the edge of her boot over a mound of dirt. "Whoever my stalker is, it's not a former boyfriend. That much I know for sure."

"I need names, Cassie. The only way to be sure is to have them checked out."

"That's a no. I don't want my ex-fiancé knocking on doors, talking to the other men I've dated. Leave it to the police."

"No one will knock on anyone's doors. I'll have Kyle do a background check and see what comes up." He pegged her with a look. This time, there was no amusement lurking in his expression. His gaze was haunted. "The last thing I want to do is come face-to-face with anyone you've dated."

He was jealous. Oh, she didn't want to know that. Her heart skipped a beat and more heat infused her cheeks. Her face must be the same shade as the barn and, for some inexplicable reason, it made her angry. "This is ridiculous. I'm not giving you names."

"Cassie..."

She planted a hand on her hip. "This isn't going to work, Nathan. There's too much history between us. If the roles were reversed, would you want to list everyone you've dated? It's absurd—"

"No one."

His answer stopped her cold. Nathan held her gaze. "I haven't dated anyone since we broke up."

Oh, heaven help her. This man could reach inside her chest and grab hold of her heart without even trying. All of her anger melted away and her shoulders sagged. She rubbed her forehead. Cassie was usually very good at controlling her emotions, but since the attack, they were all over the place.

She dropped her hand. "I've been busy with work. There hasn't been a lot of time for dating." She licked her lips. "I've been out once or twice with the local vet, Holt Adler. But it's very casual."

Why did she add that last sentence to the end of it? Wouldn't it be better to have Nathan believe she was heading into a committed relationship?

"Holt isn't stalking me," Cassie continued. "He grew up in this area, went away for college and vet school, then moved back. Never married. No kids. There's no need to have Kyle do a background check on him."

Nathan's mouth hardened. "Cassie, there's something you need to understand. Until your stalker is caught, everyone is under suspicion."

She was about to argue with him when the sound of an approaching vehicle cut her off. Nathan jumped into motion. He took a protective stance in front of her, his broad shoulders blocking her view of whoever was coming down the drive. Tension in his muscles indicated it wasn't someone Nathan recognized.

Cassie watched with increasing horror as his hand flipped up the back of his shirt to reveal a concealed handgun at the small of his back. His fingers wrapped around the weapon.

SIX

Sunlight glinted off the SUV's windshield, preventing Nathan from seeing the driver. His fingers brushed against his weapon holster, but he didn't pull his gun. Chances were, the person bouncing over the rutted dirt road leading to the house was a neighbor or friend. But Nathan wouldn't take chances. Not with Cassie's life.

He felt, rather than saw, Cassie peek around his shoulder. She swatted his arm. "It's Bessie and Eric. Stand down, soldier."

Nathan released his hold on the holster and let out a breath. "Papa Joe called me the same thing last night."

Cassie's cheeks tinged pink. "I made a rule that your name wasn't to be used after..." She shook her head, blonde hair rippling like a waterfall. "Anyway, he started calling you soldier. I guess the moniker stuck."

"You guys talked about me?"

She cast him a wry smile. "Papa Joe did. He always liked you, Nathan. That never changed."

With those parting words, Cassie strolled past him to greet Bessie and Eric. The moment the SUV stopped, Eric hopped out. He ran to Cassie and threw his arms around her. They were still hugging

29

moments later when Nathan caught up to them. Papa Joe came out of the house to join the group, Gus at his side.

"I'm glad you're okay, Eric." Cassie smiled warmly, tears shining in her eyes. "And I'm happy to see you, but you could've stayed home today."

"Wild horses couldn't keep him away," Bessie said, rounding the SUV. Mid-forties, her trim figure and bubbly personality made her seem years younger. She greeted Papa Joe with a hug. Then she surprised Nathan with one as well.

"It's good to see you looking so well, Nathan."

"You too, Bessie. Rumor has it you got married since I last saw you." Nathan had considered sending a gift but wasn't sure if she would accept it. "Congratulations."

"Thank you. David is a good man, a hard worker. He's a long-distance truck driver, so he's often away. Like now. I hope you'll have the opportunity to meet him." She backed away and patted his cheek. "Still fond of lasagna?"

He smiled. Bessie was the best cook, even better than Nathan's aunt, which was saying something. "I'd never turn down your lasagna."

Her face lit up. "Good. Then we'll have it for dinner tonight."

"Hold on, there," Cassie interjected. She had her arm wrapped around Eric's waist. "No one asked what Eric and I want for dinner. Don't we deserve a say?"

Bessie waved a hand dismissively. "You both love my lasagna. I don't even need to ask."

They all laughed. Then Papa Joe's expression grew serious. "Did Chief Garcia come by to speak with y'all this morning?"

Eric nodded. "He was upset with me."

"No, he wasn't, honey," Bessie reassured him. "Why don't you head into the barn and start with your chores?"

"The stalls have been cleaned." Cassie bumped Eric's hip with hers. "Jump right into the fun part and exercise the horses."

Eric fist pumped the air, before spinning on his heel and racing for the barn. His exuberance brought a grin to Nathan's face. "I can see why it would be difficult to keep him away. He still loves working with the horses."

"He's the best there is," Cassie said with pride in her voice. "Patient. Kind. The animals can sense his good heart and genuine sweetness. It puts them at ease. They trust him even before they trust me sometimes." Her expression hardened. "I can't believe anyone would ever attempt to hurt Eric. Makes me want to tear the man who attacked him last night apart with my bare hands."

Nathan shared her sentiment. From the looks on Bessie and Papa Joe's face, they felt the same. Not everyone in Cassie's family was blood related, but they all took care of each other. It was something Nathan had always admired.

He missed them. All of them. The hard knot of regret lodged in his chest grew. He'd been incredibly foolish to throw his relationship with Cassie away. But there was no turning back the clock. Some mistakes had to be lived with.

"Eric couldn't identify the attacker," Bessie said, drawing Nathan's attention back to the topic at hand. "He was riding home yesterday when a man wearing a ski mask jumped out of the woods and grabbed Casper's harness. It scared Eric so badly, he shut down. The rest of what happened is a blur."

Once again, Nathan had the niggling thought that Cassie's stalker was someone she knew. Eric too. Holt Adler, the veterinarian, must've been to the farm numerous times to tend the horses. Cassie didn't believe the man was capable of stalking her, but Nathan knew evil could hide in unlikely people. Kyle, his cousin, was a tech genius and a former security specialist. Doing a background check on Holt would take a day, maximum.

"Chief Garcia was disappointed that Eric couldn't provide more information," Bessie continued. "Eric's afraid he's let everyone down. I tried to talk to him about it, but I don't think it helped."

"I'll speak to him," Papa Joe said.

"He's a hero," Nathan added. "Eric pointed toward the river, which was the only way I knew where to look for Cassie. You might mention that when you speak to him."

Papa Joe's expression warmed. "I will."

Cassie glanced at her watch. "I'd better get a move on. I'm supposed to open the shelter in an hour. Bessie, do you need me to drop off pastries for the coffee shop?"

"I have them in the SUV, but I can take them—"

"I don't mind." She jerked her thumb in Nathan's direction. "I've got a bodyguard watching my every move, keeping me safe."

Forty minutes later, fresh from a shower, Nathan was balancing a collection of pastries on his lap while Cassie drove to town. The tray contained cinnamon rolls, muffins, and an assortment of cookies. His stomach growled, reminding Nathan that he'd skipped breakfast and it was nearly lunchtime. "When did Bessie start baking for the Roasted Beans?"

"Last year. I keep urging her to open a catering business, but she hasn't taken the plunge yet. Eric's autism makes it difficult. He's grown and more independent than ever, but I think she's worried he'll need her and she won't be there."

"Makes sense. She spent twenty years raising him. It's difficult to let go for most parents. I can only imagine it's more so when the child has special needs." Nathan settled against the seat and focused on the sideview mirror. No one was following them.

"How's your family?" Cassie asked, drawing his attention back to her. "You mentioned Kyle earlier. Is he stateside?"

"Yes, permanently. He got out of the military shortly after I was injured. He's the one who convinced me to move back home. My aunt and uncle are urging me to buy the ranch next door to theirs."

"You don't want to?"

"I enjoy working their land, helping out the family. But I'm not sure where I want to put my roots down yet."

His aunt and uncle were wonderful. They'd taken him in after his mother died of breast cancer during his senior year of high school. And he knew they loved him, as did Kyle. But Nathan never quite felt as though he belonged.

He didn't feel like he belonged anywhere. It'd been a large part of the reason he'd joined the military in the first place. That and a burning desire to fulfill the promise he'd made to his mother on her deathbed. He would follow his dreams and become a Green Beret, no matter what.

As if she sensed the train of his thoughts, Cassie glanced at Nathan before focusing back on the road. "Have you been to your mother's gravesite since coming home?"

"Not yet." His hands tightened on the pastries in his lap and he forced himself to loosen his grip. "I know it's something I have to do, but..."

"I know."

She did. Cassie was probably the only person on the planet who understood how painful it was to confront his mother's passing. Nathan knew she was with the Lord, but it didn't ease his grief. Some days, it felt like she'd died yesterday. He missed her deeply.

Cassie glanced at Nathan again. She cleared her throat. "If you decide to go, and want someone to go with you, I can."

Her offer touched him. But it wasn't surprising. Cassie's tough exterior shielded a heart bigger than Texas. You could be her worst enemy, but if you called needing help, she'd be there in a moment. Nathan hadn't appreciated that enough about her when they'd been dating.

"Thank you for the offer, Cassie. I'll think about it."

She nodded and turned onto Main Street. The center of Knoxville was picturesque, with a town square, tree-lined streets, and red-brick buildings. A church sat on the corner across from a hardware store, a tiny grocer, and a coffee shop. The awning on Roasted Beans was a cheery yellow. It brightened the otherwise overcast day.

Nathan climbed out of Cassie's truck. "Rain's coming."

"Sure is." She held open the door for him. "Let's grab some sandwiches for lunch and get over to the shelter before it pours."

"Sounds like a plan." Nathan carefully balanced the tray as he crossed the tile floor to the counter. The scent of coffee wrapped around him. He'd had one cup already but decided to order another with his lunch.

Cassie greeted the young lady behind the counter with a brilliant smile. They started chitchatting about the pastries. Most of the tables in the small establishment were empty. A single elderly couple sat near the window, sharing a thick slab of cake.

Bells over the door announced a new visitor. A tall dark-haired man entered. Nathan quickly assessed him. Mid-thirties, 6 foot tall, 190 pounds. No concealed weapon. His cowboy boots were scuffed, his jeans stained. There were faint circles under his eyes, as if he hadn't slept well in several nights.

Something inside Nathan pinged with awareness even before the man called out Cassie's name. Holt Adler? Any questions were extinguished the moment the stranger crossed the room and embraced Cassie. Yep, this was the new man in her life.

A rush of jealousy flew through Nathan and it took effort to keep his emotions in check. He had no right to be upset. He'd walked away from their relationship. But logic had no place where Cassie was concerned.

Nathan took a deep breath. He forced his brain to kick into gear and assess the interaction between Cassie and Holt. She'd called their relationship casual. Judging from the way the veterinarian was holding her, his feelings went deeper. Could he be frustrated by how slow his relationship with Cassie was developing? Had he become obsessed with her? Both scenarios were possible.

And it put Holt Adler at the top of Nathan's suspect list.

SEVEN

Cassie wriggled from Holt's smothering embrace. She edged away without much trouble, but he held on to her elbow. His gaze traced her form, worry drawing his brows together. "I was at the Jackson's ranch, checking on their new calf, when I heard you'd been attacked last night. Are you okay?"

"I'm fine." She should be pleased he worried about her. Holt was a handsome guy with a nice smile and a good family. Safe. Wholesome. On paper, he was everything Cassie should want.

But his touch never made her heart skip a beat.

"I'm glad." Holt seemed to sense he was crowding her personal space, because he dropped his hand from her arm. He took a respectful step back. "Are Joe and Eric okay? Mike Jackson didn't have all the details. He just knew there'd been some kind of assault."

"No one was seriously hurt, thank goodness."

Holt waited for Cassie to explain what'd happened, but she didn't feel like sharing the tale again. It was too emotionally exhausting. She offered him a weak smile instead. "How'd you know I was here?"

"It's Wednesday. You always stop in for a tuna fish sandwich on wheat bread and a coffee before going to the shelter."

"Right." A sudden case of nerves trickled down her spine. Cassie had a habit of frequenting the Roasted Bean, but it was strange that Holt knew her exact order. She didn't even know how he took his coffee.

How could she? They'd only been out twice, and both times had been for dinner. Most of their interactions had been while caring for animals at the shelter or on her ranch. Cassie couldn't even remember the last time she saw Holt in the Roasted Bean.

Was he the stalker?

She took a step back. Something in her demeanor must've tipped Nathan off because he edged closer. The security of his presence calmed the fear threatening to upend her reason. She was protected. Nathan wouldn't allow anyone to hurt her.

Cassie took a deep breath. "Holt, I'd like you to meet Nathan Hollister. Nathan, this is Holt Adler."

The two men shook hands and exchanged pleasantries. Holt didn't know Nathan was her ex. Almost no one in Knoxville did, since most of Cassie and Nathan's courtship, along with their disastrous near-wedding, happened in North Carolina. There were only a few people aware of Cassie's history with Nathan. Her family, and her best friend and coworker at the shelter, Leah.

Still, Holt must've sensed some kind of latent romantic tension, because there was a flicker of hurt in his eyes when his gaze settled on Cassie. He forced a smile. "I'm really glad you're okay. I know we haven't talked much, but if you need anything, you can always call, Cassie."

His kind words sent Cassie's mind spinning in a different direction. Holt had never given her a reason to be afraid of him. She felt terrible for suspecting him. "Of course, I know that. Thank you, Holt. Can I buy you a coffee? Or lunch?"

"No, thanks. I'm actually on my way home."

"Cassie mentioned you're a vet," Nathan said. "Hard work. Especially during springtime."

Holt nodded. "I was traveling between two farms last night, both of them on the opposite side of town from each other. But that's what it takes sometimes." He stifled a yawn. "Sorry. I'd better get home before I fall asleep right here on my feet."

Holt dipped his head to meet Cassie's gaze. "Remember what I said. Call anytime if you need something." He started backing out of the coffee shop, pointing to Nathan as he did. "Nice to meet you, Nathan." Then he waved to the elderly couple in the corner. "See you later, Mr. and Mrs. Fischer. Make sure you don't give Sparky too many doggie treats."

The bell over the door jangled as Holt exited. Cassie watched him jog down the sidewalk and disappear from view. A myriad of thoughts wrangled for priority in her mind. She was still sorting through them as she and Nathan got back into her SUV with a bag of sandwiches and fresh cups of coffee.

"Penny for your thoughts?" Nathan asked, pulling on his seat belt. He latched it with ease. Cassie's vehicle wasn't small, but Nathan's massive frame made the seat appear flimsy. His broad shoulders strained the fabric of his shirt.

She was staring. What on earth was wrong with her? Cassie tore her gaze away from Nathan and his muscles to start the vehicle. She pulled out of the parking spot. "I was thinking about what you said about everyone being under suspicion. Specifically Holt."

"He cares about you. More than you care about him."

Cassie slanted a glance in Nathan's direction. For some ridiculous reason, she defended Holt. "That doesn't make him guilty of stalking me."

"No, but he knew your Wednesday routine right down to your sandwich order. He was traveling between two farms across town, which means he could've easily stopped at your ranch to attack Eric and you." Nathan arched a brow. "Nothing I'm saying is anything you haven't already figured out. But you feel bad for thinking he could be the stalker."

"Stop that. Stop reading my mind. I don't like it."

"You have a good heart, Cassie. That's nothing to feel bad about." Nathan glanced at the sideview mirror. "Does Holt have a boat?"

Raindrops peppered the windshield as Cassie turned into the shelter's parking lot. "He does, but half of the ranches in this county have property along the river. I reckon most of them have fishing boats. The attacker could have even stolen one, for all we know."

"True. It's something to ask Chief Garcia about the next time we speak to him."

The only conversation Cassie wanted to have with the police chief was to learn they'd caught her stalker. She grabbed the coffees and exited her vehicle. A bolt of lightning ripped across the sky, followed by a window-rattling boom of thunder. Cassie hurried to locate the front door key.

The sky opened up just as she turned the lock. Cassie stumbled inside, laughing, and Nathan followed. She flipped on the lobby lights. "Two seconds more and we would've been soaked."

He lifted the takeaway bag. "Forget about us. We would've been eating soggy sandwiches."

"Yuck." She led the way farther into the building. The inner office lights were already on, since a junior staff member had come in earlier to feed the dogs and cats in their care. "We can eat in my office. Then I'll put you to work walking Bruiser. He's a pit bull, but super sweet."

"Bruiser? You're kidding. That's his actual name."

She grinned. "You'll love him. His owner was a dog trainer for the military." Her smile faded, sadness washing over her. "Unfortunately, he died in a car accident last week and there wasn't any family who could take Bruiser. That's how he ended up with us. I'm being particular about the home I place him in. I want someone who will understand his training and be capable of handling such a special dog."

Nathan arched his brows. "I'm not in the market for a pet, Cassie."

She plastered on a look of mock innocence. "I don't mean you. Heaven's no."

He grunted in reply, and Cassie bent her head so her hair would hide the twitch of her lips. She twisted the knob on her office door. Nathan would love Bruiser. She just knew it. The man needed a dog and Bruiser deserved an owner who would take good care of him.

It was strange to think that she could match Nathan with a dog and trusted him to care for the animal without question, but when it came to their relationship, she wasn't willing to bend even a little. It was part of the confusing mess she found herself in. Nathan wasn't a bad person. She'd never thought that, not even her angriest moments. But he had scarred her heart in a way that was irreparable. Some things couldn't be undone. Or forgiven.

She opened her office door and paused midstep. A sick feeling twisted her stomach.

Perched on her desk was a bouquet of red roses.

Nathan nudged her aside and entered the room. He set the takeaway bag on a chair. "Were you expecting flowers?"

"No. It must've been delivered this morning. Or maybe late last night. We close at nine on Tuesdays."

Goose bumps broke out across her skin. Deep inside, she already knew the roses were from her attacker. But she wanted to be wrong. Cassie spotted a card attached to a floral stand. She removed it and ripped the envelope open. A card fluttered out to land on her desk.

We're meant to be, sugar plum. I haven't given up on us yet.

Cassie stared at the uppercase block lettering. She'd survived a childhood racked by neglect and abuse, been abandoned by her mother at a grocery store as a teen, lived on her own in college. She was street smart. Confident. But this...it struck at an embedded fear she hadn't realized before now.

This was her safe place. Cassie could still remember the day the social worker dropped her off at Papa Joe's for the first time. The gentle rolling hills, the forest and the river, this town and the people in it...they were home. The only real home she'd ever known.

Now, she couldn't see the danger coming. It was everywhere. The stalker was stealing everything she held dear, including the one thing she'd fought so hard to protect. Her peace of mind. Trembles shook her body as a silent scream seemed to build inside her.

No. No. No.

Nathan's hand landed on the small of her back. The warmth of his palm seeped right through her thin T-shirt. "Cassie, it's going to be okay. I won't let him get near you."

His tone was firm, assured. Still, Cassie couldn't pull her gaze away from the note. Nathan put a finger under her chin and gently turned her head until she was staring into his determined green eyes. "I promise to keep you safe."

She believed him. Tears flooded her eyes. Cassie leaned into his touch until she was nestled in his embrace. She breathed in the scent of his cologne. It was warm, with a hint of leather and sandalwood. His touch, the solidness of his form, comforted her. It was familiar and dangerous. Nathan was a weakness she hadn't quite shaken from her system. The last thing Cassie needed was to survive a stalker, only to end up with another heartbreak.

She stiffened. Nathan must've sensed her tension, because he released her. Cold air replaced the warmth of his body. Cassie balled her hands into fists to stop herself from pulling him back to her.

She needed Nathan's protection, yes. But she had to draw the line at accepting his comfort.

Nathan pulled out his cell phone. "I'll call Chief Garcia. He'll want to know about the flowers and the note."

She nodded. A bolt of lightning streaked outside the office window. For a brief moment, the parking lot was as bright as a summer day, illuminating a dark form staring into her office.

Cassie screamed.

The shelter lights went out.

EIGHT

A booming rattle of thunder so deep Nathan felt it in his bones punctuated Cassie's scream. The room was pitch-black, except for the faint glow from his cell phone. It caught on the features of her face. She was pale and trembling.

Her fear sucker punched Nathan. Cassie was as tough as they came, but everyone had a limit. She'd backed away from his embrace only moments ago, but Nathan couldn't stop himself from placing a hand on her arm.

"It's okay, Cass." The familiar nickname slipped out before Nathan realized it. "The storm just knocked out the electricity."

"There was someone outside. Staring in the window."

His gaze shot to the darkness beyond the windowpane. It was impossible to see the parking lot, but the hair on the back of Nathan's neck rose. A thousand possibilities rolled through his mind as he snapped into defense mode. Had the storm taken out the electricity? Or had the stalker?

Either way, he was planning an attack. The roses, the note, appearing in the parking lot. It was designed to terrify Cassie into submission, so she would be too frightened to fight him off. But he'd underestimated his target. Already Cassie's trembles had subsided. Her hands were balled into fists, as though she was ready to punch something. Or someone.

The sound of Chief Garcia's voice filtered from the cell phone. It was frantic. Cassie's scream had cut off their conversation. Nathan lifted the phone to his ear. "We're okay, but someone's in the parking lot at the shelter. Send officers to our location now."

He hung up before Chief Garcia could say anything more. It was standard operating practice to stay on the line with emergency responders until help arrived, but this wasn't a typical situation. The glow from the cell phone announced their location to any hostile outside. Nathan switched it off.

"We need to move from this room." He blinked, letting his eyes adjust to the darkness. The outline of Cassie's desk formed, along with her chair. Her door was the only entrance and exit from the room. They were sitting ducks. "Where are the exits to this building?"

Nathan mentally berated himself for not doing recon the moment they'd arrived at the shelter. It was a mistake he wouldn't make again.

"The front entrance leads to the parking lot, as does the one at the end of the hall." Cassie's words were clipped and whispered. "There's another emergency exit in the back of the building. It leads to the street, but you have to go through the dog enclosures to get there."

Not ideal. The dogs would bark announcing their presence, but going into the parking lot wasn't an option. Nathan weighed his choices. They didn't need to exit the building, just have an escape route accessible. Back of the building it was.

He pulled his weapon and then took Cassie's hand. Her skin was soft, and when she wrapped her fingers around his, Nathan's heart stuttered. No other woman had ever made him feel like she did. A simple touch and he would lasso the moon if she asked. It was uncontrollable. And terrifying.

He wasn't good enough for her. Had never been. But he could protect her. The skills gained through his career with the military and as Green Beret had prepared him for this moment. Nathan would do anything—anything—to keep Cassie safe. He prayed it wouldn't come to that.

Rain battered the windows and roof as Nathan led Cassie to the doorway. He squeezed her hand. "Hold on to my belt and stay right behind me. We're going to a more secure location."

Her features were shrouded in the dark, but she released his hand and grabbed hold of his belt loop. Nathan undid the safety on his weapon. The handgun molded to his hand, a natural extension of his body, as familiar to him as breathing. He kept it pointed at the ground as they exited the office. No one else should be in the building besides them, but the police had been called, and he wasn't sure what the policy was on approach. They might not announce their presence with lights and sirens.

The red glow from an overhead emergency exit sign at the end of the hall was the only illumination. Several more rooms jutted out, doors open, their interiors black holes big enough to hide a person. Had the stalker gained access to the building? It was possible. The doors were locked, but the shelter didn't have a security system.

All the more reason to get Cassie to a location they could escape from.

Chances were, the stalker was counting on them going to the nearest exit, passing all of those dark offices in the process. Nathan led Cassie in the opposite direction. He swiveled his head, keeping his attention and senses heightened for any noise or movement. His boots didn't make a sound on the tile floor. Cassie's hand tightened on his belt loop. She pressed herself against his back, matching him step for step.

Nathan edged toward the rear of the building. The sound of a dog howling reached his ears. Another joined in, followed by a third barking. Poor things must be terrified, caged up and in the dark. A short hallway led to the door. Rather than turn, leaving his back exposed, Nathan stepped in reverse, pushing Cassie toward it.

Glass shattered in the lobby. The sound of rain grew louder. Nathan's heart rate jumped in response.

Time to speed their exit up.

He lifted his weapon while increasing his pace to the door. His focus was so intense, it took several steps before he realized Cassie was shoving against his back. She leaned in close to his ear. "Leah is scheduled to work the front desk today, and she's set to arrive any minute. I can't let her walk into this."

He paused. "My job is to protect you."

"Not at the expense of others. Leave me here. I'll be fine."

"Absolutely not. You'll be alone and vulnerable. The stalker could've broken the glass in the lobby to draw me outside while he circles around back."

"I have a solution for that problem." She reached around him to grab a leash hanging from a row of pegs. Then she hurried to the door.

Seconds later, they were in the holding room. The howling was deafening, bouncing off of the concrete floor and walls. Without a word, Cassie beelined for a cage in the rear. She spoke in a hushed tone to the dog inside, quickly undoing the latch and hooking the leash to the animal's collar. Dim light filtering in from the long windows along the back wall provided illumination. Nathan's breath caught as a massive pit bull exited the cage. His square head accentuated a powerful jaw and muscular body.

Bruiser.

Smart thinking on Cassie's part. The dog had been trained by an expert, which meant he could attack on command. Bruiser sniffed Nathan's boots and then licked his hand.

Cassie whispered a word in German, and Bruiser's demeanor

changed immediately. He took up a protective stance in front of her. She squared her shoulders. "Go, Nathan. I'm safe here. Please. I don't want Leah to get hurt."

He couldn't ignore her logic or her pleading. The stalker's attack on Eric proved he would harm others in order to get to Cassie. Nathan spun on his heel and went back into the hallway. The door clicked closed behind him.

He paused, straining his ears to listen beyond the sounds of the rain and the dogs howling. There. A scuffling noise to the left, in the direction of Cassie's office. Nathan moved silently toward the sound. He peeked around the edge of the corner.

A dark form stood at the other end of the hallway. A poncho-style raincoat covered most of his body, the hood pulled low to hide his face.

Cassie's stalker.

"Don't move," Nathan commanded, lifting his weapon.

The figure whirled, the red glow of the emergency exit glinting off the gun in the intruder's hand. Nathan ducked. A bullet whizzed by, chipping off a piece of the corner. Dust from the sheetrock rained down. Footsteps pounded over the tile floor.

He was escaping.

Oh, no, you don't.

Nathan sprang from his hiding place just as the stalker shoved open the emergency exit and slipped outside. With a growl of frustration, Nathan followed. He used his body to press the handle and bolted into the parking lot. Rain soaked him in an instant. His gaze swept the lot, searching for any sign of the man.

Nothing.

Refusing to give up, Nathan bolted for the edge of the building. The intruder had come in the front door. Maybe he'd parked on that side of the building too. His boots pounded against the concrete. His still-healing leg protested the rapid movement. It was sore from yesterday's encounter, and once again, Nathan was pushing beyond his limitations. But there wasn't a choice. He couldn't let Cassie's stalker get away.

He rounded the side of the building in time to see a dark-colored truck roaring through the parking lot. It headed straight for Nathan.

He dove out of the way. Pain vibrated along his shoulder and hip as they collided with the asphalt. He rolled, crashing into the broken front door of the shelter. Shards of glass littering the entrance cut into his skin. The truck bounced off the sidewalk and then sped into the street. Nathan sprang to his feet, desperate to catch a glimpse of the license plate, but it was too late.

The vehicle was gone.

NINE

Cassie swiped a mop across the lobby floor, attempting to clean the tsunami of water that'd poured in from the broken door. The rain had dissipated to a drizzle. Several officers bustled back and forth, gathering evidence. One dusted for fingerprints, another carried the bouquet of roses from her office. Cassie would never again look at roses—or plums—without feeling sick to her stomach. It angered her. What other seemingly harmless item would the stalker ruin?

"Cassie, what are you doing?" Leah Gray, her best friend and coworker, came from the break room. Her curly hair bounced with every step. Thick-framed glasses drew attention to her gorgeous chocolate-brown eyes and instantly made her appear smart and capable. Which she was. In one hand, she carried a bottle of water. "Sit down. We can take care of that later."

"It's better if I have something productive to do." Cassie's gaze drifted toward Nathan and Chief Garcia. They were in deep conversation. She should go over and listen in but just for a moment. Cassie needed a break from the chaos.

Mopping. Mopping was something she could handle.

"Here." Leah offered the bottle of water, and then her gaze

followed Cassie's. "Nathan Hollister. Now that's a blast from the past."

"Tell me about it." Cassie uncapped the water and sipped. She wasn't one to talk about her love life with people, but Leah had always been a fantastic listener. Her friend never judged and gave excellent advice. Even if it wasn't something Cassie wanted to hear. "Part of me wants to send him packing to Siberia. The other part..."

She couldn't bring herself to say the words out loud. Even now, Nathan's presence was like a homing beacon. Her attention couldn't stop drifting his way. His hair was still damp from the rain, and his soaked shirt clung to every ridge and muscle on his chest. The man didn't have an ounce of fat on him.

Good looks were one thing, but coupled with Nathan's bravery, his supportive gentleness, the way he'd listened and responded to her fears for others...it was intoxicating. She'd missed it. Missed him.

Standing in the holding room with Bruiser after hearing the gunshot echo through the building had been some of the worst moments of her life. Nathan could've died. And it would've been her fault. Not directly. But she was still responsible.

"You loved him, Cassie. You were going to marry him. Those kinds of feelings don't turn off just because you want them to."

She sighed. "I know." Cassie lowered her voice. "He apologized. He said walking away from our wedding was the biggest mistake of his life."

"Duh. I could've told him that four years ago." Leah adjusted her glasses. "Guess that's why you want to pack him off to Siberia. An apology coupled with saving your life puts things in a confusing place."

Relief uncoiled in Cassie's stomach. Some part of her must've been afraid no one would understand. "Yes."

Leah gave her a sympathetic look. "I know it's hard to be around Nathan, but his presence in your life right now is for a reason. Be patient. The Lord works in mysterious ways, and His timing isn't always ours."

"You know I don't pray anymore."

"Since when?" Nathan's question interrupted their conversation. His brows drew down, creating a crease on his forehead. "Sorry. Couldn't help overhearing that last part. Since when did you stop praying, Cassie?"

"It's been a while." She didn't want to have this conversation with him. Mostly because it'd been Nathan leaving on their wedding day that pushed her into a crisis of faith.

Commotion near the front door caught her attention. Dwayne Booth, the contractor Cassie hired to build the new barn on her property, stepped inside. She'd called him to replace the window on the front door.

"Dwayne, thanks for coming so quickly." Cassie set the mop against the wall and moved to intercept him, thankful for the interruption.

Mid-forties, Dwayne was tall and muscular from years of working on construction sites. His auburn hair was mussed and in need of a cut. A pencil stuck out from behind one ear and the dust from wood shavings coated his plaid shirt.

Cassie didn't know him well, even though they'd gone to high school together. She and Dwayne had run in different circles. He'd been away from Knoxville for many years, like her, only recently moving back with his family. His wife was a professional wedding photographer and his kids were in elementary school. They were an adorable family. And the work Dwayne had done on her new barn was exceptional. Cassie was thrilled to have an experienced contractor living in town. It would make expanding her nonprofit easier.

She introduced Dwayne to Leah and Nathan before showing him the busted front door. "I think it just needs a new pane of glass, but I'd like you to check the lock as well and make sure everything is okay."

"Sure thing." Dwayne glanced around the lobby. "Can't believe someone broke in here. I mean, for what? To steal a dog?"

Cassie didn't correct his assumption. She didn't have the mental or emotional energy to explain about her stalker. It was too terrifying.

Chief Garcia, speaking on his cell, caught Cassie's eye and waved her over. "Excuse me, Dwayne."

She crossed the room to join the chief, Nathan at her side. Chief Garcia hung up his phone. "We got a break. The clerk at the flower shop remembers the order. They don't have cameras, but she got a good look at the guy's face. Caucasian male, around six feet, with dark hair and eyes. Didn't seem like a local, according to her."

"Why is that?" Nathan asked.

"Maple Jennings has been running her flower shop for the last forty years. She's also a member of the city council. There's not a person in three counties she doesn't know. If she says the guy's not a local, I believe her."

Cassie nodded. The chief was right. Mrs. Jennings would recognize someone from the area. "When were the flowers ordered?"

"First thing this morning. He wanted the roses delivered immediately and paid extra—in cash—to have Mrs. Jennings close up the shop to do it." Chief Garcia blew out a breath. "Since she got a good look at him, I'll have a state sketch artist make a composite. It may take a few days though."

A few days? Cassie had been attacked twice within twenty-four hours. She didn't have a few days at this rate.

Nathan must've been following her chain of thought because he said, "I don't think I need to say this, but the faster we get this criminal off the streets, the better."

"I don't disagree. Trust me. I'm doing everything I can, but I don't control other state agencies. And we aren't big enough to have a sketch artist on staff." The chief rocked back on his heels. "I have one more piece of news to share. Nathan, you were spot on about the boat. The attacker stole it from a neighboring ranch up the way from Cassie's. We recovered it this morning."

Cassie's gaze jumped back and forth between the two men. "Is that significant?"

"Could be. The stolen boat and the fact that Mrs. Jennings didn't recognize the man could mean that your stalker isn't from here. You moved to Knoxville a few months ago. It's possible he followed you from North Carolina."

Cassie wasn't sure whether to be relieved by this new tidbit of information or not. The frown on Nathan's face indicated he didn't agree with Chief Garcia's assessment. She waited until the police chief walked over to speak to one of his officers before asking, "What do you think, Nathan?"

"Chief Garcia may be correct." Nathan met her gaze. "But if your stalker is a local, I don't think he'd risk showing his face at the flower shop or using his own boat."

Horror sank into her with sharp fangs. The only thing worse than having a stalker was having two. "You think there's more than one person involved? That the stalker hired someone to order the flowers for him."

Nathan nodded. "It's an easy way to confuse the police, keep them busy chasing a suspect that won't lead anywhere. I've mentioned my opinion to Chief Garcia, and he agrees with me, but the evidence is limited. The best lead they have is the man at the flower shop." He placed a reassuring hand on her arm. His palm was warm, his touch gentle. "Don't worry, Cassie. Chief Garcia will chase down his leads, and I'll be working mine. Together, we'll find out who's behind this."

"When? And what will happen in the meantime?" She bit her lip. "You could've been killed today, Nathan."

He chuckled. "Not even close. In case you haven't noticed, Cass, I'm pretty hard to get rid of."

She found herself grinning back. "I've noticed."

Cassie leaned against the wall next to Nathan. She put her head on his shoulder and watched the commotion in the lobby. A headache was brewing at her temples, and her stomach churned. Despite Nathan's reassurances, she was worried. How long could this go on? The weight of her responsibilities pressed down on her shoulders. Papa Joe, the shelter, the ranch, her rescue horses...

She inhaled sharply. "Nathan, if the stalker is willing to hire someone, that means my family could be at risk even if I'm not on the property. He's already proven he'll hurt others to get to me."

"I've already thought of that. Chief Garcia is stationing an officer on the property for today. But it's not a permanent solution. For that, I have a few friends that can help us out."

"I don't have the money to hire a security team."

"Don't worry." He grinned at her, the dimple in his cheek flashing. "The guys I know work for food."

TEN

Nelson's Diner was situated off an old country road. Pot holes the size of dinner plates littered the parking lot and crooked blinds hung in the windows. The scent of greasy fresh fries and onions perfumed the air.

Cassie wrinkled her nose as she climbed out of the SUV. "This is where you meet your friends?"

"Every Wednesday night." He snagged her hand, gently tugging her across the parking lot. "Don't judge. This place may not look like much, but it has the best pie in Texas. Guaranteed."

The dessert was only part of the draw. Nelson's Diner was quiet most weeknights, providing Nathan and his buddies a chance to talk and swap stories without worrying someone was going to overhear. All of them were injured in combat, which cut their careers short. The transition to civilian life could be difficult to navigate, and they'd formed the group to support each other. It'd started off small—Nathan, his cousin Kyle, and Jason Gonzalez—but had grown slowly over the last year to include others.

Nathan held open the door for Cassie. Harriett greeted them with a smile big enough to smush her cheeks. Her hair was steel gray, but she had more energy than most people half her age. She and her husband, Nelson, had built the diner in the eighties. They were both old enough to retire, but as Harriett said, what else would they do. Cooking for weary travelers and locals gave them a reason to get up in the morning.

"You brought a friend with you." Harriett beamed, seemingly as pleased as if she was Nathan's own mother. She swiped her hands on the apron tied around her ample waist and focused on Cassie. "Welcome, sweetie. So glad to have you here."

"Thank you, ma'am." Cassie extended a hand toward the older woman and introduced herself.

Harriett grabbed a couple of menus and patted Nathan's arm. "The whole crowd is waiting for you. Come on back."

"Heya, Nathan." Nelson waved from the opening between the front counter and the kitchen. Stains marched across his apron and the chef's cap over his head hid his bald spot.

Nathan waved back. "Got any pecan pie left?"

"Saved you a piece."

A glass display on the front counter held a wide assortment of homemade pies in tin trays. The scent of them filled the diner. Some pies were cut, since customers could order an entire tin or just a slice. Flaky crusts browned to perfection encased filling enticing enough to make any person's mouth water. Cassie's steps slowed. Her eyes lit up, and a smile tweaked the corners of her mouth.

Nathan chuckled and leaned in close to her ear. "Told you. Best pies in Texas."

She turned her head to meet his gaze, warmth shining from her deep brown eyes. Nathan's chest tightened. Man, the woman was beautiful. It was like a sucker punch to his solar plexus every time she smiled. The scent of her shampoo tickled his nose. She smelled of strawberries and sunshine. It was familiar, and yet still heady and intoxicating.

His gaze dropped to her lush mouth, inches away from his. The diner seemed to fade away. Nathan knew he should take a step back, but every muscle in his body refused to move. He couldn't. Not when it came to Cassie.

She was his person. His soul mate, if such a thing existed. Leaving her four years ago had been the hardest thing he'd ever done. Nathan could still remember standing in his tux, staring at his cell phone, reading the text message from his commander. Wheels up in thirty minutes.

As a Green Beret, his missions were classified and he could be called away at any moment. Even on his wedding day. Nathan had known right then and there that he and Cassie would never work. Oh, they'd talked about his job and the strain it would put on their relationship. But Cassie wasn't the kind to walk away from something hard, even if it made her miserable.

Being with Nathan would've made her miserable. She needed reliability. Honesty. Support. None of which Nathan could provide as long as he was a Green Beret. He couldn't discuss his missions with her, couldn't promise to be there if she needed him, and would be missing for months at a time. The secrets and distance would've eaten away at the love they shared.

He'd left Cassie to protect her. His intentions had been in the right place, but his execution had been abysmal. *What-if* haunted his dreams and most of his waking hours as well. Nathan desperately wanted a second chance, but there was a higher probability of seeing flying unicorns than convincing Cassie that her heart was safe with him.

Kissing her would be a giant mistake. His job was to protect Cassie, and he couldn't do that if he made her uncomfortable by pushing for something more than friendship. The delicate balance they'd created over the last few days was too precious to risk.

Nathan tore his gaze from her lips and forced himself to take a step back. Cassie blinked, a pretty blush rising in her cheeks. She shook her head and, without a word, hurried to catch up to Harriett. Nathan followed.

The sound of male voices grew louder as they approached the table in the rear. Five sets of eyes turned in their direction and the conversation died.

Cassie stiffened. She hated being the center of attention, always had. Nathan placed a hand on her back to remind her she wasn't in this alone. "Guys, this is my friend Cassie."

A round of *heys* followed. Nathan introduced each man at the table. "Tucker Colburn, former Army Ranger. Logan Keller, Air Force medic. Walker Montgomery was a Navy SEAL." He gestured toward his cousin. "And that ugly mug I'm sure you recognize."

Cassie's grin widened as Kyle rose from his chair. She embraced him. "Long time, no see, Kyle. How's your family?"

"They're great." He patted her back in a brotherly gesture. "My parents send their regards. My mom made me promise to tell you that their house has an open door policy. Stop by anytime. They miss you."

"I'll have to take them up on that."

Nathan pulled out a chair for Cassie, but before she could sit, the last member of their group arrived. Jason Gonzalez was a former Marine who'd been injured in an IED explosion. His service dog, a German shepherd named Connor, strolled by his side. Addison Foster, her auburn hair tied back into a ponytail, held Jason's hand. The couple looked happier than ever, something Nathan was thrilled to see. Addison's life had been threatened last year, and Jason had protected her from several close encounters with a killer. They'd fallen in love during the experience and had gotten married last month.

Normally, Addison didn't come on Wednesday nights. Not that the men didn't adore her. They all did. But her presence would've changed the dynamic of their unofficial support group. Tonight, however, Nathan had called Jason and asked him to bring Addison.

Having another woman at the table, especially one who'd recently had her life threatened, would make Cassie feel more comfortable about the dinner and accepting help.

For the two hours, the conversation at the table was lighthearted and fun. Cassie's peals of laughter warmed Nathan's heart. He kept catching himself just staring at her, his insides doing cartwheels. A thousand memories flooded his mind. Fighting over the last bit of popcorn in a movie theater, stolen kisses at her front door, strolling hand in hand through a park, long conversations while staring at the stars. He'd missed her far more than he'd allowed himself to admit to.

After dessert, once Harriett had refilled everyone's coffee mugs, Kyle glanced at his watch. "I hate to break up this good time we're having, but I've got to bug out soon. Nathan, you want to give us an update on the situation."

He quickly summed up the threats against Cassie. Around the table, every man's expression hardened. All of them had taken an oath to serve and protect. None of them were active military anymore, but it didn't erase what was ingrained in their DNA. Even Addison looked ready to join the battle. No surprise there either. She was a lawyer who worked on behalf of abused women and couldn't tolerate a bully of any kind.

"Cassie's family needs protection," Nathan summed up. "The man after her has already proven he'll hurt people close to her to send a message. Any volunteers?"

"Count me in," Jason said, without hesitation. The other men all nodded in agreement.

Some of the tension in Nathan's muscles loosened. He hadn't doubted his friends would help, but it was nice to have the confirmation. He glanced at Cassie. "Problem solved. You've got five of Uncle Sam's finest at your service. Six, including me."

"Guys, I can't thank you enough." Her hand tightened around her coffee mug. "And if any of you decide to back out, there are no hard feelings. Truly."

"Nonsense." Tucker scraped the last bit of apple pie left on his plate and then grinned at Cassie. "We've been up against some of the most terrifying terrorists on the planet. Your stalker won't have me shaking in my boots any time soon." His gaze shifted to Nathan. "What do we know about this guy anyway?"

"Not much." He ran through the possible scenarios. "It could be someone from North Carolina, but I'm still leaning toward a local. None of the stalking happened until after Cassie moved home."

"I did a primarily background check on Holt Adler," Kyle said. "No red flags that I could find. But I need more time to dig deeper, find some of his ex-girlfriends and talk to them."

Cassie opened her mouth, an objection written all over her face, but Nathan placed a hand on her arm, stopping her from saying anything. It was uncomfortable for her to implicate anyone, but the situation was dangerous enough they had to cut to the chase. A thorough background check was the only way to rule Holt out.

"Do it as discreetly as possible, Kyle." Nathan shared a knowing look with his cousin. If Holt was the stalker, they didn't want to tip him off.

His cousin nodded. The group spent a few more minutes tossing around ideas about motives and potential suspects, but nothing new came of it. Then they set up a rotating plan of protection. No one in Cassie's family would be left vulnerable. Finally, everyone got up from the table and said their goodbyes.

The cool night air felt good as Nathan escorted Cassie to his truck. She hooked her arm through his. "Thank you, Nathan, for arranging this."

Her praise warmed him straight through. A romantic relationship was out of the question, but maybe, just maybe, a friendship would be possible. "You're welcome, Cass. I'm glad to help."

They reached his truck. Nathan opened the door for her, but Cassie didn't immediately get inside. She rested her palm on his chest. "Addison told me about what happened to her last year. She said you helped save her life. That you were shot in the process."

He shrugged. "She was in trouble and needed help."

A beep came from her purse, cutting off their conversation. Cassie pulled out her new cell phone. They'd replaced it this morning, since her old one was lost in the river during the stalker's first attack. The glow of the phone played across the delicate features of her face.

She went pale.

"What is it?" Nathan asked, dread skirting down as she tilted the screen so he could read the message.

No one can keep us apart. Why can't you see it? You're mine, sugar plum. Always have been and always will be.

The phone beeped again with another message.

I'm warning you. Get rid of your bodyguard while he's still breathing. Don't make me angry, sugar plum. You'll regret it.

ELEVEN

The specific threats against Nathan plagued Cassie's thoughts the next morning. She went through her morning chores on autopilot, and although she'd planned to work with her latest rescue horse, she decided to skip the training. She wasn't in a calm headspace. Horses were sensitive animals and training required firm authority. Cassie's tension would ruin any progress she'd made previously. It wasn't worth the risk.

The sky was still cloudy and gray, but the rain had stopped. She leaned against the fence. The yards of green pasture bracketed by thick woods was picture perfect. Normally, the sight of it would calm Cassie's nerves. Today, she felt too on edge.

Starlight trotted over, sniffing her jacket pockets before nudging her shoulder. She laughed, despite her moodiness. "You always know when I'm carrying sugar cubes."

"He's a smart horse." Nathan strolled toward the fence line, Bruiser trotting at his side.

The pit bull's tongue lolled out in happiness and Cassie could've sworn he was smiling. He'd been miserable in the shelter, so she'd brought him to the ranch as a foster. It was temporary. Just until they could find the right home for him. Leah had actually suggested it, insisting it was a win-win for both of them. Bruiser would be happier and he could provide another layer of protection. Papa Joe's dog, Gus, was like a member of the family, but his poor eyesight and age made him a bad guard dog.

So far, Leah's advice had been sound. Bruiser was thrilled to be on the ranch. In fact, he hadn't left Nathan's side all morning.

Cassie reached into her pocket and gave Starlight a treat. She kissed his nose before stroking him. "He is a smart horse. The best."

"Did you rescue him?"

Cassie's heart did a flip as Nathan leaned against the fence next to her. Every fiber of her being was aware of him, from his muddy boots to the warmth radiating from his skin. It was becoming increasingly harder to ignore the attraction between them. Like an itch between her shoulder blades she couldn't scratch.

That Nathan was doing all he could to keep Cassie and her loved ones safe...well, it made it increasingly difficult to stay mad at him too.

"Starlight is a rescue horse, the first one I ever trained." She fed him another sugar cube. "After college, I worked for a nonprofit that saved all kinds of animals—not just horses. Goats, pigs, you name it."

Cassie loved that job. She'd gained knowledge and experience that'd helped her tremendously now that she was running her own nonprofit. "Starlight's previous owner had abused and starved him. He was so sick, we weren't sure he would make it. Now, look at him. Happy and healthy." She rubbed the bridge of his nose. "I couldn't bear to part with Starlight after the training, so I adopted him myself. Brought him to Texas with me when I moved."

She gave the horse a last pat on the shoulder before dusting off her hands. "I need to check on the progress of the new barn. There are some final touches I wanted to speak to Dwayne about."

"I'll join you." Nathan fell into step beside her.

Papa Joe and Eric were on the porch, shelling peas. Cassie waved, and Eric grinned. He waved back. Bessie was probably inside, cleaning and working on lunch. Everyone had been sticking close to the house since the attacks. It was frustrating—Cassie didn't want to be a prisoner in her own home—but until the police could find her stalker, it was the smartest option.

She slipped her hands in her jacket pockets. It wasn't particularly cold, but the lightweight garment helped her hide the handgun tucked in the holster at the small of her back. As much as Cassie resisted carrying a weapon, the attack at the shelter proved she was in serious danger. Her stalker would keep trying. She needed to be prepared to defend herself, and possibly others.

"Nathan..." She struggled to put her feelings into words. Cassie had never been very good at complicated relationships. Nothing about this situation with Nathan was simple, but she couldn't escape the fact that as difficult as this was for her, it couldn't be any easier for him. He'd arrived on the ranch to have a conversation and was drawn into a life-and-death situation.

She paused in the field and Nathan did too. She took a deep breath, raising her gaze to his. "Thank you. For everything. I haven't treated you kindly at times, but you've continued to protect me and my family. It means a lot to me—"

He held up a hand to stop her. "Any hard feelings you have toward me are justified. I hurt you, Cassie. I know that."

There was no judgment in his gaze, only understanding and warmth. And something more...something that made her heart pick up speed and drew her closer to him. She knew that look. Desire. Wanting. It caused a flutter of butterflies in her stomach. She longed to step into his arms. But the question she desperately wanted to know burned the back of her throat and kept her feet planted in place.

Why?

Nathan had explained that leaving Cassie on their wedding day had been the biggest mistake of his life, but he hadn't actually explained why he'd done it. Did it even matter? Cassie wasn't sure. But it scared her to ask the question, so she swallowed it back down.

He stared out across the field and then focused back on her. "I am sorry, Cass. I hope you can find it in your heart to forgive me."

She knew his words were genuine. It didn't take away all of her pain, but it blunted the edges. "I'm working on it."

He laughed, the dimple in his cheek winking. "That's fair."

She found herself grinning back. Although things between them weren't completely sorted, it felt like they'd reached an equilibrium. Nathan fell into step beside her as they continued to the barn. Bruiser pranced ahead, tail wagging, periodically turning around to make sure they were still headed in his direction. His happiness was infectious. The tension melted from Cassie's shoulders.

"How long will it take to complete the new barn?" Nathan adjusted his ball cap to shade his eyes from a sunbeam breaking through the clouds. "It looks nearly complete."

"It is. There are a few details left, but I could technically house horses here now. Leah and I are planning a fundraiser for next month. We'll have food. Carnival attractions for the kids. There will be a bouncy house over there." She pointed. "Face painting. Horse-back riding. I wanted it to be family friendly, but there will be an educational booth, too, explaining about rescue horses. Everyone will get a chance to learn about what we do. We'll also collect the names of individuals interested in adopting the horses once they've been through our program."

Excitement bubbled up inside her. Cassie was determined to make her rescue horse facility a success. In a perfect world, no one would abuse any animal, but sadly, that wasn't the case. Her ranch would be a safe place for the horses that'd been mistreated.

"Your entire face lights up when you talk about it, Cass. I can understand why after meeting Starlight and some of the other horses you've rescued." Nathan gestured to Bruiser. "Even he's thrilled to be here. I know the fundraiser and your nonprofit will be a huge success. It sounds wonderful."

His words touched her. Nathan had always been supportive of her ideas and passion projects. She'd missed having him in her corner.

"Thanks, Nathan. My hope, if this year is successful, is to turn the fundraiser into a yearly event." Cassie grasped the handle on the barn's main door, but before she could pull it open, Nathan placed a hand on her arm. He lifted a finger to his lips, indicating she should be quiet. Then he pointed to the ground.

Boot prints.

Cassie's heart stuttered. No one had been out this way since last night's thunderstorm. Had her stalker been on the property?

Was he still here? Inside the barn?

The boot prints circled around the side of the building to the rear entrance. They were large, definitely caused by a man. Nathan removed his weapon in one fluid motion from underneath his shirt before following them. Cassie fell into step behind him, removing her own handgun from its holster. A bead of sweat dripped down her back, but a quiet stillness filled her core. She refused to give in to fear. Nor would she leave Nathan to face her stalker alone.

The rear door to the barn was cracked open. Tree leaves rustled. Cassie's gaze scanned the area. No one was hiding in the woods behind the barn. The dirt road was muddy from the recent rains. It wasn't the main road onto the property and was rarely used.

A shadow drifted over the opening to the barn, followed by a scuffling sound. Someone was definitely in there. Cassie's muscles tensed. She adjusted the hold on her weapon. Her palms were slick. She wasn't a coward by any means, but these attacks were terrifying in their frequency. All she wanted was to be left alone.

Nathan glanced in her direction, an unspoken question in his eyes. Was she ready? Cassie nodded. He grabbed the handle and swung the door wide open. Leading with his weapon, he ducked inside. "Put your hands in the air right now!"

Heart in her throat, Cassie followed.

TWELVE

The blood roared in Nathan's ears as he entered the barn, gun raised.

Dwayne Booth, the contractor, yelped as his clipboard clattered to the ground. He shot both hands into the air, palms facing forward. His eyes were wide with fright. "D-d-d-on't shoot me. Please."

Nathan lowered his weapon but didn't holster it. He tamped down on the adrenaline racing through his veins. It was a struggle to keep his tone even. "What on earth are you doing in here?"

"T-t-the barn needs some final touches. The crew is scheduled to come out in a few days, so I wanted to take a look around myself and make notes about what needs to be done."

"We didn't see you drive onto the property." His gaze narrowed. Dwayne appeared genuinely shocked, but Nathan wouldn't take anything for granted. Cassie's stalker was smart, which probably also made him a good actor. "Why didn't you use the main road?"

"It's shorter to use the rear entrance, but I wasn't expecting it to be so muddy. I parked my truck back aways." Dwayne's gaze shot to Cassie, who'd appeared at Nathan's side. "I texted to let you know I was coming."

"I left my phone in the house," she murmured.

She'd been bothered by the stalker's texts last night and likely hadn't wanted to risk facing another one this morning. Nathan released a long breath. Dwayne's reasons for being on the property were valid and his explanation about using the rear entrance made sense. The man was still standing with his hands in the air. The clipboard he'd dropped had landed face up. A list was visible. Nathan couldn't read the scrawled writing, but it looked nothing like the stalker's block lettering from the note included with the roses yesterday.

He holstered his weapon. "I'm sorry to have frightened you, Dwayne. There's been some trouble on the property."

He lowered his hands. "I heard. Chief Garcia spoke to me yesterday while I was replacing the window at the shelter. He explained Cassie has a stalker." Dwayne shot her a sympathetic look. "The chief wanted to know if anyone from my crew had showed a particular interest in her."

Cassie stiffened. Nathan edged closer to her, a silent reminder that she wasn't in this alone, even while he mentally kicked himself. Why hadn't he considered someone from the construction crew was responsible? The new barn had taken weeks to build. "What did you tell him?"

"I hadn't noticed anything unusual, but that doesn't mean much. I can't swear Cassie's stalker didn't work for me. Most of the men I employ are regular staff, however I hire extra temporary workers from time to time. They're often men just passing through town, looking to be paid in cash."

"How many of the temporary workers assisted with the barn?"

"About a half a dozen." Dwayne bent to collect his clipboard from the ground. "I provided Chief Garcia with a list of names."

"What are the chances some of those names are fake?"

He grimaced. "Pretty likely. At least, from the temporary workers. Like I said, they're interested in quick money and I don't do background checks. The regulars are a different story. Those are local men and many of them have worked for me since I started my business last year."

Nathan stifled a groan. The suspect list was growing by the second, and although it'd been a few days since the initial attack on Cassie, they were no closer to figuring out who her stalker was. "If you could provide that list of names to me, Dwayne, I would appreciate it."

He felt like a heel asking for something after nearly scaring the man out of his work belt, but Dwayne simply nodded. He handed over his clipboard. "Write down your email. I'll send the list of names the moment I get back to the office."

Nathan scrawled his contact information on the paper. Chief Garcia would do an initial search, but he had limited resources and staff. If Cassie's stalker was among the men who worked on the construction crew, Nathan didn't want to overlook it. Kyle could do a deeper dive into each individual.

He handed the clipboard back. "Thanks, Dwayne. I really appreciate it."

"It's nothing. Anything I can do to help, just ask." Dwayne's gaze landed on Cassie. "I'm really sorry you're having so much trouble. It ain't right. My wife had a stalker when we lived in Mississippi. A coworker from her job. Scared the living daylights out of her."

Cassie hugged herself. "I didn't know that. Was the man arrested?"

Dwayne nodded. "He's still in jail, but that's the reason we decided to move. My wife wanted a fresh start. Please, don't mention I told you. Sally's doing a lot better now, but she has some bouts of fear every now and again."

"Of course."

Guilt washed over Nathan. He removed his ball cap and raked a hand through his hair. "Let me apologize again for busting in here with my gun drawn. Really sorry for scaring you, Dwayne."

"That's quite all right. You're protecting Miss Miles and there's nothing wrong with that." He lifted the clipboard. "Is now a good time to go over my list, or would you rather we do this another day?"

"Now's fine." Cassie took a deep breath and smiled.

The two of them began talking about the repairs. Nathan opened the rear barn door wider to let in more sunlight. He scanned the tree line and the pasture, but the only movement came from a squirrel running across the grass to a nearby oak.

Nathan's friend, Tucker, was doing patrols on the property, but there were over 100 acres. It was impossible to be everywhere at once. Maybe they should increase the number of men? Dwayne's presence in the barn was proof that their system wasn't foolproof.

Bruiser trotted over. Nathan patted the pit bull's head. "Aren't you supposed to be a guard dog? You missed all the excitement, buddy."

Bruiser's eyebrows shifted, as if he was trying to understand what Nathan was saying. The dog was adorable. His brindle coat shone as he plopped in the grass, resting his head on his paws, to watch the squirrel. Ranch life suited him.

For a moment, Nathan considered adopting Bruiser, as Cassie had suggested. But then he rejected the thought. He didn't know where home was yet, and it wouldn't be right to commit to a dog without having his life sorted.

Nathan's phone rang. He glanced at the name flashing across the screen before answering. "Hey, Kyle, what's up?"

"I've got an update for you on Holt Adler. Spoke with a couple of his former girlfriends. According to them, he's intense but harmless. Long story short, the man checks out."

Nathan leaned against the doorframe. Inside, Cassie was pointing to a stall door, deep in conversation with Dwayne. Her expression was animated. Whatever she said made the contractor laugh.

A pang of jealousy rippled through Nathan. It didn't make logical sense. Dwayne was married, with a wife and children. He'd shown no romantic interest in Cassie. No, Nathan was reacting to Kyle's comments about Holt Adler. That man definitely had his sights on the beautiful woman standing several feet away. And Nathan didn't like it. Not one bit.

Of course, he also had no right to say a thing about it. He'd been the one to blow up their relationship. It was a miracle some other man hadn't already married Cassie. She was one in a million. She also deserved to be happy.

"Hello?" Kyle said. "Nathan, are you there?"

"I'm here. Just thinking. Holt's ex-girlfriends called him intense. In what way?"

"He called a lot, sent flowers, and discussed marriage early in the relationship. The word overeager was how one ex described him. But the minute she broke things off, Holt left her alone. And he was never disrespectful. Both women felt bad for him. Holt wants to get married, but neither was the right fit for him."

Nathan grunted. It certainly wasn't a crime to want to get married. Nor did it sound like Holt was the stalker. "We need to widen the net of possibilities. I'm going to send you a list of names later on today. Cassie is having a new barn built on her property. Someone from the construction crew could be responsible for the attacks."

"How many names are we talking about?"

"Don't know. Ask some of the guys to help you. We need to move fast on this."

"You got it."

"Thanks, Kyle." Nathan hung up. His mind whirled with possibilities. The construction crew was a good lead, and it should be followed up on. But Cassie had grown up in Knoxville. Could her stalker be someone from her childhood? A school crush, for example? He hadn't considered it before, since the stalking started recently, but it was worth asking about.

A few minutes later, Dwayne left. Cassie joined Nathan in the doorway of the barn. She scratched Bruiser behind the ears. "The crew will finish the barn in the next couple of days. I told Dwayne to make sure they use the main entrance to the ranch."

"Good." Nathan frowned. "Cassie, I've been thinking. We assumed your stalker was someone you met recently, because that's when the attacks happened. But that theory could be wrong. Can you think of anyone from your past who could be stalking you now? Not necessarily a boyfriend. It could be someone else. A childhood friend, maybe?"

She inhaled sharply. Her gaze lifted to meet Nathan's. "There is someone. We need to speak to Papa Joe."

THIRTEEN

The kitchen table was covered with dirty dishes and remnants of the lunchtime meal. Cassie took Nathan's plate and added to her own before handing them to Bessie. The scent of fresh coffee dripping into the carafe filled the space. From the living room came the indistinct murmur of the television. Eric was watching a movie.

Papa Joe sat across the table, booted leg propped on a chair. His shoulders slumped. "Jace Hayes. You think Jace could be involved in this mess?"

"I don't know." Cassie had waited until lunch was over before bringing up the topic. She knew it would be a sensitive subject for Papa Joe. "I hope not. But Nathan asked me if someone from my past could've been triggered by my return home and started stalking me. Jace was the first person to come to mind."

"Who is he?" Nathan asked, his gaze shooting between Cassie and her grandfather.

"A foster kid I took in when Cassie was sixteen." Papa Joe sighed. He ran a hand over his face. "Jace was close to eighteen. He'd been removed from his mother's custody after she was sent to jail for drug possession. No one in his extended family wanted to take him."

"Why?"

"He was a troubled young man. Prone to fighting and difficult behavior. I knew the social worker for this area well. I wasn't a foster parent, but I'd filled out all the required paperwork to be one so I could care for Cassie. Anyway, the social worker asked if I'd be willing to take in Jace until he graduated from high school. It would only be for a few months and it could mean the difference between him having a high school diploma or not."

Cassie's heart broke for her grandfather. He'd been trying to do the right thing by helping a troubled teen. There was no way for Papa Joe to know how terrible that decision would be.

"Jace took a special liking to me," Cassie said. "At first, he treated me like a little sister, but as time went on, his actions turned more possessive."

Nathan's jaw tightened. "Possessive how?"

"He told Papa Joe lies about my friends so I wouldn't be able to see them, followed me around at school, and wouldn't allow me to walk home by myself. Things increased from there."

She shivered, remembering the way Jace had slowly taken over her life. It'd been insidious. Why hadn't she thought of him when these incidents started? Probably because she blocked out that chapter of her life. Cassie was good at that. It was a skill she'd learned during her childhood, when survival meant ignoring the bad, otherwise it might crush her.

These attacks had thrust her back into that survival mode. It felt like she was floundering on rough seas with no safe harbor in sight. Even Nathan was dangerous to her well-being. He'd broken her heart once before.

She wanted to protect herself from being hurt again. For the last four years, she'd worked to block Nathan from her thoughts. The last few days demonstrated just how futile her attempts to purge him from her system were. It made Cassie wonder if she was truly helping herself by blocking out everything that hurt. Maybe she'd been lying to herself the entire time.

But what other choice did she have? Giving her feelings full rein would leave her curled up in a ball lying on the floor. That wouldn't help anyone, least of all her.

"Jace was also jealous of Cassie's relationship with Eric." Bessie removed the carafe from the coffee maker and brought it to the table. "I noticed Eric was acting strange, but it took weeks before he finally confessed that Jace had threatened to hurt him."

"Eric wasn't the only one." Cassie's stomach churned as the memories came flooding back. "Once I fell in the hallway in high school and Dwayne was nice enough to help me up. There was nothing to it. We barely knew each other since we ran in different circles. But Jace threatened to kill Dwayne if he ever touched me again."

"Sounds like the making of a stalker." Nathan's jaw tightened. "How long did all of this go on?"

"Too long," Papa Joe said. His expression was weary. "Cassie told me what was happening, but I didn't understand the seriousness of the situation. I thought Jace was merely looking out for her. Being protective. I spoke to him several times, explained that Cassie was old enough to make her own decisions about her friends and so on. But then Bessie told me he'd threatened Eric. I started asking Cassie more questions and paying closer attention."

"It wasn't your fault, Papa Joe." Cassie patted his wrinkled hand. Despite his age, it was still strong from working on the ranch. "You see the best in everyone. It's one of the reasons I love you so."

Bessie passed out coffee mugs filled to the brim and set a plate of homemade cookies in the center of the table. "I missed it too. Jace was excellent at the art of manipulation. He had all the adults convinced he was turning his life around."

"Be that as it may, I still feel responsible." Papa Joe sighed again. His hand drifted down to pet Gus. The loyal dog never left his side.

"I ordered Jace to stay away from Cassie. The next day, I found my Debbie..."

Tears shimmered in his eyes. Cassie felt her own throat tightening in response. Her grandfather had the kindest heart of anyone she'd ever met. She cleared her throat. "Papa Joe's favorite coonhound, Debbie, had been tortured and killed."

Nathan's gaze swung to Cassie. His eyes were hard. "Jace?"

She nodded. "It was the only person who could've done it."

"Although he denied it," Bessie pointed out. She tossed her braid over her shoulder. "Empathically. The kid was a good actor. Jace nearly had me believing he was innocent."

Papa Joe sighed again. "After that, I asked the social worker to remove Jace from my home. It nearly killed me to do it. I still think of him from time to time, pray for his well-being."

Nathan leaned forward. "Why didn't any of you mention Jace as a possible suspect before?"

"This all happened so long ago." Cassie's hand tightened around her mug. The warmth seeped into her palm but did little to remove the icy feeling nestled in her core. "Jace was placed with another foster family in a different city. I never heard from him again."

"I got reports from the social worker from time to time," Papa Joe said. "Jace got his GED and left the state to work on an oil rig. Last I heard, he was doing well. This was about six years ago, a'course. After that, the social worker lost contact with him." He frowned. "I hate to think he has anything to do with the current threats against Cassie. But I have to admit, based on his time living with us, it's possible."

Cassie's mind raced. "Jace knows the property since he used to live here. He's familiar with Eric and his limitations." It'd been foolish not to consider the possibility of Jace's involvement before. But she honestly hadn't thought about it until Nathan asked about people from her past. "And he's dangerous."

"Hold on." Bessie lifted a hand. "I'm not a fan of Jace, but we haven't seen or heard from him in over ten years. Isn't it farfetched to think he's come back to hurt Cassie? I mean, why now?"

She had a point. Cassie shifted in her chair. Was she so desperate to locate her stalker that she was jumping to conclusions? She hated the idea of accusing an innocent man of wrongdoing. "Bessie's right. Jace left town a long time ago. I don't even think he visits his mother."

"She still lives here?" Nathan asked.

Cassie nodded. "She was released from prison a couple of years ago. Before we talk to Chief Garcia about our suspicions, it might be worth visiting Mrs. Hayes. She may know more about her son's whereabouts. He could be deceased for all we know."

Nathan was quiet for a long moment. "You're right. Chief Garcia is running down other leads. Before we muddy up his case further, we should see if Jace is even a viable suspect. I can have Kyle—"

"No." Cassie straightened her shoulders. She was tired of feeling hunted. This was something she could do to take back some measure of control. "I want to speak to Mrs. Hayes. I need to hear her answer the questions."

"You want to know if she's lying."

Cassie nodded. Nathan hesitated, his lips clamping shut as he seemed to weigh the options and risks. She held her breath. She didn't want to fight him on this, but it was important to her. Cassie was going crazy sitting around waiting for her stalker to make the next move.

Nathan searched her gaze. Worry lurked in his eyes, but something in her expression must've convinced him. He sighed. "Okay, Cass. We can talk to her together."

FOURTEEN

Linda Hayes lived in a cute one-story house in a neighboring town about thirty miles from Knoxville. Her front yard was a riot of color. Flowers of every size and shape bloomed in an intricate and beautiful display. A hip-high fence, complete with a fairy-tale style gate, finished the design.

A woman was in the center of the yard. She wore gardening gloves and a wide-brimmed hat. Jace's mom? The woman resembled the photographs Nathan had found online. Mid-forties and curvy, with a wide forehead and thin lips.

He'd done a brief background check on Linda and her son. Both had a criminal record. Linda had a past history of drug abuse. Her last arrest had been ten years ago. Jace had followed in his mother's footsteps but with a more violent twist. Assault with a deadly weapon, attempted murder, and drug dealing. Jace had spent most of his twenties in and out of prison. He'd been released last year, skipped his parole, and was currently a wanted man.

Questions flitted through Nathan's mind during the drive to Linda's house. If Jace was Cassie's stalker, why come back and attack her now? It was a risky move. Then again, Jace had nothing left to lose. The minute law enforcement caught him, he'd be in prison for skipping parole. For a long time. If Cassie was an obsession for him, and had been for the last decade, Jace might have decided this was the right time to make his move.

Nathan scanned the quiet neighborhood street before opening the truck's passenger side door. Everything was quiet. He offered Cassie a hand. Her gorgeous lips tipped up into a smile as her fingers slid against his palm. A jolt rippled through him. Her skin was soft and the scent of her perfume—strawberries and sunshine—teased his senses.

Mentally, Nathan knew he should be careful about getting too close to Cassie again. She'd been very honest about her feelings, but that didn't stop him from hoping she'd change her mind and give their relationship a second chance. It was foolish. He would only get his heart broken, but Nathan was willing to accept the risk. She was worth it.

Cassie released his hand once her feet were on the ground. Nathan shut the passenger side door and fell into step beside her as they approached the house. The garage door was open. One vehicle was inside, a late-model sedan. Muddy rain boots, sized for a woman, sat next to a wheelbarrow. Tools with pink handles lined a peg board. If Jace was living with his mother, there was no indication from the exterior of the house.

"Hello." Cassie waved to the woman in the garden from the gate. "Are you Mrs. Hayes?"

The woman peered at them from under the wide brim of her hat. "I am. Can I help you?"

"We hope so." Nathan undid the latch of the gate and waited for Cassie to pass through first before following. "We'd like to speak to you about your son, Jace."

Her gaze narrowed and irritation made her nostrils flare. "Are you cops?"

Interesting. Nathan wondered how many police officers had

come looking for Jace. Probably quite a few given his wanted status. "No, ma'am. My name is Nathan Hollister."

Her gaze raked over him, suspicion evident in the flattening of her mouth. "You look like a cop."

"He's former military." Cassie stepped forward, drawing Linda's attention to her. She smiled disarmingly. "It gives him that tough appearance, but I promise we aren't cops. I'm Cassie Miles. Jace lived with my family for a brief period while he was in high school."

Linda's expression morphed into one of shock and then happiness. "Of course." She rose. "Cassie, I recognize you now. Jace always spoke so highly of you. My goodness, you're as beautiful as the photograph he showed me."

It took all of Nathan's self-control to keep a pleasant smile plastered on his face as Linda embraced Cassie. His fingers twitched, wanting to drag her away from the older woman. A sick feeling settled in his gut. Bringing Cassie here might have been a terrible idea.

The hair on the back of Nathan's neck stood on end. He glanced behind him at the house. Nothing stirred. Yet it still felt like someone was watching them.

Linda released Cassie and laughed. "I know we've never met, but I feel like I know you. Have you heard from Jace? I've been so worried about him. The police have come half a dozen times looking for him. Have they been in contact with you too?"

"No, ma'am." Cassie took a step away from the other woman but kept a gentle smile on her face. "Actually, I was hoping you'd been in contact with Jace."

Linda tilted her head, sadness clouding her expression. "Hasn't he told you? We had a big fight shortly after he got out of prison. I haven't seen or heard from him since."

"No, he didn't mention it. What was the fight about?"

Cassie's acting skills were top notch. Nathan was impressed with her ability to put Linda at ease and keep the conversation moving. Especially since there was something about the woman that made his spidey senses tingle. Cassie had to be feeling the same thing. She'd always been good at reading people.

"The fight was about *nothing*." She waved her gloved hand as if shooing away a pesky fly. "But you know my Jace. He takes things personally."

Cassie nodded. "Do you know of any way I could contact Jace? Any friends he might call? It's important that I speak with him."

"About what, dear?"

"There was an argument between my grandfather and Jace," Cassie said smoothly. "Papa Joe recently had a heart attack, and he asked me to locate Jace. He wants to apologize for his part in their disagreement."

Linda pressed a hand to her cheek. "Oh dear. Jace never mentioned a word of this."

"When's the last time you spoke to him?"

"It must've been a year ago. Jace talked as if the two of you were still in contact. It was all Cassie this and Cassie that."

Nathan's stomach tightened. There was no question Jace was obsessed with Cassie. Could he have been stalking her for years without Cassie realizing it? It was a horrible proposition to consider. "Do you have a contact number for him?"

Linda shook her head. "No, his cell has been disconnected. And I'm afraid I don't know any of his friends. Jace didn't like to bring them around much when he was growing up. I'm so surprised you haven't heard from him, Cassie. You were the only person he ever talked about. I thought for sure you two would get married." Linda eyed Nathan. "Is this your husband?"

"No. He's just a friend."

"Oh. Well, would you like to come up to the porch? Have some iced tea?"

That pinprick of awareness wouldn't leave Nathan. He glanced over his shoulder at the house. Again, nothing moved. "We should get going, Cassie. There's some repairs to do at the ranch." Nathan met Linda's gaze. "Maybe we can come back another time."

"Of course." She smiled brightly. "Whenever you want."

Linda linked her arm through Cassie's and led her along the walkway to the gate. "Now, if you hear from Jace, can you please tell him to contact me? I've been distraught about our fight. We said some harsh words to each other and I hate to think he's still thinking about them."

"Of course."

"And whatever you do, don't talk to the police. They have it out for Jace." Linda lowered her voice as if a police officer was hiding in the bushes. "My boy has been unfairly treated. Most of the charges against him were bogus. Jace is smart and successful. It makes others jealous. They always want to knock him down."

Nathan mentally rolled his eyes. Jace was a career criminal whose actions had brought the police to his doorstep, not the other way around.

Cassie simply patted Linda's hand. "Oh, I know. I never believed a word of the things people have said about him."

"Of course you wouldn't." Linda beamed. "Jace was right about you. You're a sweetheart. Please come back and see me when you have more time. I'd love for us to get to know each other better."

The way Linda was looking at Cassie gave Nathan the creeps. There was definitely something off about Jace's mom.

Was she secretly in contact with Jace? It was a possibility. It was hard to believe Linda would ever argue with her son about anything. She seemed to think the world of him. Normally, that wouldn't rub Nathan the wrong way, but in this particular instance, it pinged his instincts in a negative way.

Cassie detangled herself from Linda's embrace and said goodbye. Nathan followed her to the truck. The back of his neck heated. It was as if Linda's gaze were boring a hole in his skin. He glanced behind him.

The expression on her face chilled him to the bone. Hatred oozed from her. But it wasn't at Cassie. No, her focus was solely on Nathan.

She wanted to kill him.

FIFTEEN

Cassie stroked Bruiser's back as she scrolled through Jace's social media on her laptop. His profile was public, so his photographs and friends were searchable. Not that it helped much. He followed and interacted with hundreds of people. In between his bouts in prison, Jace spent most of his time online. Cassie recognized several of the names on his friends' list. They were people from their high school.

She clicked on the last photograph he'd shared. Jace was standing in a field, a lit cigarette dangling from the fingers of his right hand. His black hair was long, curling around the collar of his T-shirt. The years in prison, and the methamphetamine drug habit, showed in the old scars on his face. He'd also bulked up since the last time Cassie saw him. Tattoos decorated his bare arms and neck. Another change.

The share date on the picture was one day before he failed to show up for a meeting with his parole officer. Cassie focused on the details of the field Jace was standing in, but the area didn't look familiar. Or rather, it was too generic. It could be any empty field in rural Texas.

The back door opened and Cassie tensed until she heard the familiar footfall of Nathan's boots. He appeared a moment later. His gaze swept over Cassie and then landed on Bruiser nestled next to her on the couch. The pit bull had his head in her lap. He looked up at her with adoring eyes.

"You're spoiling that mutt." Nathan's mouth quirked.

Cassie covered Bruiser's ears as if to shield him from the conversation. She mock scowled at Nathan. "Hush, you. I'll spoil him as much as I like. He's had a rough go of it." She stroked his silky ears. Maybe it was all in her imagination, but she sensed the dog was missing his previous owner. "Bruiser needs a little TLC. If that means letting him sit with me on the couch, then that's what we're going to do."

Nathan grunted and settled himself in Papa Joe's recliner. The fabric of his jeans strained to cover his muscular thighs. He'd forgone his usual ball cap, and his hair stood on end as if he'd been raking his hand through it. He leaned his head back and then sighed.

He was tired. A wave of tenderness swept over Cassie. She had the urge to reach out and stroke his bristled cheek before kissing the worry from his expression.

Dangerous thoughts. They were coming with more frequency and becoming harder to ignore. The walls around her heart were cracking with every minute spent in Nathan's presence. Her stalker needed to be caught. And soon. Otherwise, Cassie might give in to this heady attraction she couldn't manage to control.

"What are you working on?" Nathan asked without opening his eyes.

"I'm studying Jace's social media, hoping it'll help us figure out where he's hiding out."

"Any luck?"

"No." She bit her lip. Cassie hated to add to Nathan's troubles, but there was no way to avoid this discussion. "I'm beginning to think Jace isn't my stalker."

Nathan's eyes popped open, and he sat up straight. "Come again?"

She turned the computer screen so that it faced him. Cassie then pointed to the photograph. "Jace is a smoker. And not a casual one. He's holding a cigarette in almost every photo of him since being released from prison a few months ago." She scrolled through the pictures so Nathan could see the images for himself. "The man who attacked me didn't smell like cigarettes. Not even a bit."

"Are you sure?"

"Positive. It's something I would have noticed and remembered." Her nose wrinkled. "I hate the smell of cigarettes. My mom was a smoker."

Nathan was quiet for a long moment. "It's not enough to rule him out, Cassie. I still think Chief Garcia should investigate Jace. But we should call and mention this to him tomorrow morning."

"Agreed." She closed the laptop and set it on the side table next to the lamp. Cassie ran her hand over Bruiser's head. "Did Dwayne send you the list of construction workers?"

"Yep. Kyle and the guys are going through it. So far, nothing's popped." He drummed his fingers on the armchair. "We're doubling up on patrols around the property. Logan and Walker will be here in a little while to take the night shift. Jason will come in the morning."

Nathan was worried. She was too. It felt like they were on the edge of their seat, waiting for the stalker to make another move. "Make sure they know there's an open-door policy. Coffee, food, even to take a nap on the sofa if they need."

That comment brought a smile to Nathan's face. "Don't speak so fast. You saw how those guys ate at dinner. Everything but the silverware disappeared."

She laughed. "Bessie loved it. She spent twenty minutes planning breakfast, lunch, and dinner for tomorrow. She's excited to have so many mouths to feed."

Silence descended, each of them lost in their own thoughts. It felt comfortable. Cassie adjusted Bruiser's collar. The pit bull cocked one eye open but didn't move from his place on her lap. "Speaking of sleeping on the couch, I may not be able to convince Bruiser to let me go to bed."

Nathan chuckled. "Serves you right for spoiling that dog." He lifted his gaze to meet hers. His expression grew serious. "Cass, there's something I've been wanting to ask you. Why have you stopped praying?"

She sighed. Cassie had known this would come up at some point. Papa Joe had introduced her to the Bible and church, but it'd been while dating Nathan that her relationship with God deepened. Until it all fell apart...

She fiddled with Bruiser's collar. "I've always struggled with my faith, but these days, it feels like God doesn't listen or care at all."

"Why do you think that?"

The question angered her. She leveled a warning look in his direction. "Do you need a list? I'm being stalked by a madman, for starters. Papa Joe has a heart condition that he refuses to take care of. My fiancé left me on my wedding day. My mother abandoned me when I was a kid. I could go on, but this isn't a pity party."

Despite the heat running through her veins, Cassie gently removed Bruiser's head from her lap. "I should go to bed. I'm tired."

She rose from the coach, but as she passed by Nathan's chair, he gently grabbed her wrist. "Cass...don't run away from this conversation. It's too important."

"There's nothing to say."

He rose from the recliner. "I disagree. You and I spend too much of our time not talking about the hard stuff. We buried it, both of us. Put smiles on our faces and tried to move past it, but here we are. Both hurting."

Inexplicably, tears flooded her vision. She couldn't hold back anymore. It was killing her. "You left me, Nathan. No explanation. Just a note saying that you were sorry and that you couldn't marry me." She forced herself to raise her gaze until she was looking him in the face. "Why? What did I do wrong?"

"You didn't do anything wrong." Nathan cupped her cheek, his thumb swiping at the tear trailing across her skin. "You were perfect, Cass. I was the problem."

"I don't understand."

"No, you don't. Because I never told you." He released her and went to the window. With one finger, he shifted the blinds and stared outside. The moonlight played with the powerful lines of his face. "It was my dream to become a Green Beret. Since I was a little kid, it was all I could talk about. And then I met you."

Pain vibrated in his voice. Cassie had the urge to cross the room and comfort him, but she didn't want Nathan to stop talking. "I always supported your career."

"You did." He let the blinds fall back to the window and faced her. "Do you remember I couldn't take leave for our wedding day?"

She nodded. Nathan had just become a Green Beret. The timing was awful to squeeze in a wedding, but Cassie hadn't cared about a honeymoon or the flowers or even a fancy dress. All she'd wanted was to marry the man of her dreams.

"That day, moments before I was set to marry you, I got a text from my commanding officer." Nathan's voice was hollow. "We had thirty minutes to report."

She inhaled sharply. "Kyle never told me that."

"I asked him not to. It's hard to explain, but in that moment, reading that text from my commander, I realized things weren't going to work. You loved me, Cass, and you would've accepted my career without question." He held her gaze, his dark eyes haunted. "But it would've hurt you in ways I can't even imagine."

Nathan drew closer. "The secrets between us—the missions I couldn't talk about, the things I'd done—were just the tip of the iceberg. What about the times I couldn't be there for you? Support you? There would be times we'd agree to do something, even mundane things like go out to dinner, and I'd disappear from the restaurant without a word because I'd been called away on a mission."

She shook her head. "We talked about this. I knew what I was getting into."

"Talking and living are two different things, Cass. My career would've delivered a thousand tiny cuts that would've destroyed us."

"So you did it with one blow?" Hurt roiled through her, coloring Cassie's words. She jabbed a finger into his rock hard chest. "You didn't even give me a chance. You bailed on us, Nathan."

He captured her hand gently in his. "I did. But would you have listened if I'd tried to explain?"

Nathan's question caught her off-guard. The diatribe swirling inside her went still as the truth of his words smacked her. What would she have said? That she loved him; that it didn't matter.

But did it matter?

Before she could answer, Cassie's cell phone rang. It was resting on the coffee table. Her blood ran cold when she saw the number was private. The stalker.

Pulling away from Nathan, Cassie scooped up the phone. Her finger trembled as she used an app to record the conversation. Chief Garcia would want to hear it later. Then she answered the call. "Hello."

"You need to send your bodyguard away, sugar plum." His voice was mechanical and cold. Creepy. "He's no good for you."

Cassie's gaze shot to Nathan's. He placed a hand on her back, a simple touch to reassure her of his presence. But the stalker's words confirmed what she'd suspected. Nathan was a target and he could be killed while trying to protect her.

She swallowed the lump in her throat. "You need to leave me alone. I don't love you. Do you understand? We aren't in a relationship—"

"We're meant to be, sugar plum. You'll see soon enough. Get rid of the bodyguard like I told you, before you lose everything you hold dear."

His threat sent shivers through her. Cassie gritted her teeth against the fear threatening to rise up and swallow her whole. Her hand tightened on the phone. "Listen you..."

A light flickered outside the window. Unnatural light. Cassie gasped, dropping the phone and racing to the door. Nathan yelled her name, but she paid him no heed. She flung the back door open. Her heart stuttered.

The barn was on fire.

SIXTEEN

Smoke poured from the barn. Flames licked up the side of the weathered wood from the hay bales, which had already been engulfed by the fire. The horses, frightened and trapped in their stalls, clambered against the wood doors. Nathan's mind snapped into problem-solving mode. Within seconds, he'd assessed the risks and dangers. The stalker had laid a trap, of that he was certain, but there was no way Cassie would stay in the house. Not while her horses were in danger.

Lord, help me protect them all.

Nathan raced across the yard, beating Cassie to the barn doors and flinging them wide open. Smoke accosted him, making his eyes tear. He pointed to the stalls closest to the door. "Get these horses out and then get back to the house. I'll get the rest."

He didn't wait for her to respond. Nathan lifted his shirt until the fabric was over his nose and mouth. Using the light of the flames to guide him, he went deeper into the burning building. The heat singed the hairs on his arms. Horse hooves beat against the stall doors. The animals were frantic.

Rage swelled inside Nathan. Most of these horses had already been through traumatic incidents—beatings and mistreatment. They didn't deserve to be terrorized by a lunatic with an agenda. Nor did Cassie. Nathan didn't consider himself a violent man, but the strength of his convictions was being sorely tested.

He reached the stall farthest from the opening and closest to the fire. The handle was metal. Too hot to grasp with his bare hand. Forgoing his own safety, Nathan dropped the shirt from his nose and mouth. Then he removed it.

His lungs seized as the smoke assaulted them. Coughing, he wrapped the fabric around his hand and then quickly unlatched the stall door before shoving it open.

Starlight burst out, eyes wide with terror. The flames were close enough to confuse him, the smoke thick enough to blind him. Nathan shoved the horse's head toward the open barn doors and then smacked his flanks. Starlight took the hint. He bolted from the barn, running right past Cassie into the pasture.

Nathan quickly set to work, freeing the other three horses trapped in the barn while keeping an eye on Cassie. She released a palomino mare without a problem, but when she got to Casper's stall, she struggled to undo the latch. Nathan sent his last horse into the field and then joined her. Urgency nipped at his heels. Something was coming. He could feel it. "What's wrong?"

Her face was red from the heat. Soot covering her forehead and cheeks, mingling with the sweat trailing from her hairline. "The latch is stuck."

He gently pushed her out of the way and grasped the metal. Using all of his strength, Nathan tried to open the stall door. It refused to budge. Wiping the tears from his eyes caused by the smoke, he examined the latch. It'd been bent. Sabotaged.

God, no.

Casper rammed against the wood. It shuddered, but the stall door was too heavy for the animal to break down. If they didn't get him out soon, he'd die. Heart pounding, Nathan spun away from the door.

There was a crowbar somewhere...he'd seen it the other day. "I'll get Casper. Get back to the house."

"The barn—"

"It's not worth your life! Cassie, please!"

She hesitated and then nodded. Nathan waited long enough to see her turn toward the barn door before wading through the smoke to find the crowbar. Papa Joe's work bench came into view. An assortment of tools were scattered across the wooden plank. Nathan passed over them, his mind racing to remember where he'd seen the crowbar.

There! It was leaning against the wall. Nathan wrapped his hand around the tool and then marched back to Casper's door. The flames were growing rapidly, eating their way through the old wood with precision. Popping and crackling filled the air. The roof groaned, and a beam fell, smashing into Papa Joe's work bench.

Nathan stood stunned for a moment. If he'd taken two seconds more to locate the crowbar...

Thank you, God.

There was no time for a prayer longer than that. Every second counted.

Nathan wedged the crowbar under the stall latch and shoved. The metal screeched as it gave way enough for the door to be opened. Nathan threw the crowbar aside and shoved the stall open. Casper needed no encouragement. The horse burst out and raced for safety.

Nathan followed. Movement caught his eye a moment before he exited the barn.

Cassie. She was bent over a basket on the floor, her hand shoved underneath a small gap in the boards. Next to her, a tabby cat cried plaintively. Muffin. She'd appeared last month, pregnant and hungry. Papa Joe and Cassie had tried to take her into the house, but the cat refused, repeatedly escaping to live in the barn. They finally gave up and made a space for her with a soft bed. Her kittens were only a few weeks old.

Nathan growled. Frustration balled his hands into fists, but he dropped to Cassie's side. Several kittens were tucked in the basket, tumbling over themselves. Their eyes were open, but they were still wobbly on their feet.

Cassie glanced at him, panic in her eyes. "There's one wedged in the wall. I can't reach it."

The woman was going to get herself killed trying to save every animal in the place. Nathan's frustration grew, but it wasn't Cassie's fault. Her selflessness was something to admire. Truth was, if he'd remembered Muffin and the kittens, Nathan wouldn't have left them either.

He lay down on the floor and shoved his hand between the boards. Heat from the flames burned his exposed skin. Sweat and soot ran into his eyes. Nathan blinked it away, focusing on feeling around inside the wall for the kitten. "Come on, come on."

His fingers brushed against soft fur. He grasped the kitten and pulled. She popped free.

Nathan placed her in the basket with the other, grabbed Muffin, and helped Cassie to her feet. She held the basket by the handles. They raced for the door, the smoke fading as the sweet smell of fresh air took its place. Nathan wanted to stop and fill his lungs, but there was no time. That urgent feeling in the pit of his stomach kept his feet moving.

He held on to Cassie's arm. She stumbled, nearly dropping the basket, and he righted her. "You okay?"

She sucked in a breath. A coughing fit overtook her. Nathan set Muffin inside the basket with her kittens and then took it from Cassie. She needed a hospital. He changed direction, away from the house and toward his truck parked behind Cassie's vehicle. Paramedics would take time. It was better to drive her himself.

A whine filled the night air, growing louder in intensity. Nathan's gut clenched. He scanned the dark sky even as his pace increased.

"W-what's that?" Cassie choked out her voice hoarse.

"A drone."

Nathan shoved Cassie behind her extended-cab 4x4 just as the object came into view. It was professional grade, large enough to carry a weapon, and heading straight for them. Nathan pulled his own handgun, but the drone was too small and the lighting too poor for him to shoot with accuracy.

A burst of light blasted from the drone. Bullets slammed into the truck's windshield, sending glass shards flying. Nathan threw himself over Cassie.

More bullets pinged against the metal as the drone continued shooting.

SEVENTEEN

Cassie clutched the basket of kittens against her chest, doing her best to protect them, even as Nathan shielded her. His strong arms created a cocoon of safety. He smelled of pine and soot and sweat. The whine of the drone was drowned out by the sound of her own rushing heartbeat. Terror streaked through her.

Not for her own safety. For Nathan's. There was no doubt he was the target of this attack. The stalker had warned her.

"Get under the vehicle." Nathan's breath brushed against her cheek. He rolled, pointing his weapon at the drone, and fired. The whirling didn't stop, but it retracted. Was it flying away? Or just backing off to prepare for another assault?

Cassie's muscles felt like jelly. She shoved the basket under the truck and followed suit. The kittens meowed in protest, even as their mother tried to gather them together in the basket. Muffin had to be terrified, judging from her wide eyes and laid-back ears, but she wouldn't leave her young ones.

Nathan pressed his cell phone into Cassie's hand. She quickly dialed 911 and answered the dispatcher's questions. Police were on the way.

The whirring grew louder. Fresh adrenaline streaked through Cassie. Nathan had taken a protective posture in front of her. She grabbed the belt loop on the back of his jeans with her free hand. "What are you doing? Get under the truck."

He ignored her command, the stubborn man. Nathan thought he was invincible. But he wasn't. The drone, controlled by her stalker, was aiming to kill. He wasn't interested in hurting Cassie—at least, not this way. His aim was to eliminate her bodyguard. "Nathan! Please!"

Bullets pinged off the truck, reverberating loudly in Cassie's ears. She screeched and covered the cats with her arms. Nathan's cell phone skittered away. Rocks from the dirt road bit into her cheek. Water dripped onto her neck, and belatedly, Cassie realized she was crying.

The slap of the screen door cut through all the noise around Cassie like a punch to the chest. Some part of her must've instinctively been listening for it.

Papa Joe.

From her vantage point under the vehicle, his feet were visible. No boots, just socks and the bottom part of his pajama pants. The shooting must've woken him. Cassie's heart clenched tight. The stalker wouldn't hesitate to kill her grandfather. She scrambled out from the other side of the truck. "Papa Joe, no!"

The drone whirred louder.

Papa Joe pumped his shotgun. He lifted it, took aim, and fired. The drone spiraled through the air, landing a short distance away in the pasture. Nathan, weapon drawn, ran toward it. Probably to disarm the horrible thing.

Cassie sagged against the bullet-ridden truck. Her grandfather hobbled down the steps of the porch. He was supposed to be wearing his orthopedic boot but didn't sleep with it on, and clearly hadn't thought to grab it in his rush to come to their aid.

"Are you okay?" Papa Joe embraced her.

Tears flowed down her face unabashedly as she clung to her grandfather. "I'm all right. Thanks to you." She pulled back, offering him a watery smile. "That was good shooting, Papa Joe."

He smiled, the wrinkles at the corners of his eyes deepening, and lifted his weapon. "Not much can withstand a shotgun blast."

Sirens wailed in the distance. Nathan came around the corner of the truck. He carried his handgun with one hand and the drone with the other. His undershirt was black with ash, his jeans torn and dirty. Every inch of bare skin was covered in dirt, grass, soot. But he was alive.

Cassie's tears started again as she stumbled toward him, wrapping her arms around his solid form. The sobs were uncontrollable, no matter how much she tried. A testament to the depth of emotion she'd tried to keep hidden, even from herself. She cared for Nathan deeply. Breaking up, and the last four years apart, hadn't changed that.

"You're okay, Cass." Nathan's arms encircled her, but he couldn't hug her well because of the items in his hands. "It's over."

"I wasn't worried about me, you big oaf." She backed away and lightly slapped Nathan's chest. It was like touching warm granite. "He was aiming for you."

Nathan's mouth curled up at the corners. He planted a kiss on her forehead. "I told you, sweetheart. I'm not that easy to kill."

Sirens wailed louder as police cars flew up the dirt road of their ranch. Hours later, Cassie's property was filled with men. A police officer took Papa Joe's statement in the living room, while another organized the CSI unit alongside Chief Garcia. Nathan's buddies had also arrived. Jason and his dog were guarding Bessie and Eric at their house. Logan and Walker were patrolling the property. Kyle was speaking quietly with Tucker and Nathan at the kitchen table.

Cassie soothed her nerves by making coffee and sandwiches. Bruiser followed her every step, as if he sensed how frazzled her emotions were. Or maybe he was as unsettled by the fire, bullets, and people as she was. Muffin and her kittens were tucked away in Cassie's bedroom. The barn was completely destroyed, but the horses were fine. Everyone was safe. Something she was incredibly grateful for.

The back door opened and Chief Garcia strolled in. He removed his cowboy hat, revealing uncombed hair and bloodshot eyes. Cassie set the plate of sandwiches in the center of the table. "Coffee, Chief Garcia?"

"Please, Cassie." His eagle-eyed gaze swept over her. The chief was exhausted, but he didn't miss a thing. "My officers told me that y'all refused to be seen by the paramedics. Sure you don't need medical attention?"

"I'm fine. My throat is sore, but it's nothing that won't pass." She poured him a cup of coffee and set it on the table before pulling out a chair.

Nathan handed her a paper plate already loaded down with a sandwich. Their fingers brushed and warmth rippled through her. He smiled, the dimple in his cheek winking. "If you don't grab one of these for yourself, they'll all be gone."

She glanced around and laughed. Every single one of the men, including the chief, was eating. Tucker finished the sandwich in three bites, then reached for another. He grinned. "Great food, Cassie. Thanks."

"I'm sure it's more tasty than an MRE." She shuddered. Meals-ready-to-eat were offensive to her taste buds.

Kyle chuckled. "MREs aren't that bad. Just add hot sauce and everything tastes better."

Nathan gently shoved his cousin. "You put hot sauce on literally everything." His nose wrinkled as if he'd smelled something foul. "I've seen you even put it on pancakes. Now that's gross."

A collective *ewwww* came from almost everyone at the table.

Kyle shrugged. "Don't knock it till you've tried it."

"That's a hard pass from me." Chief Garcia took a long sip of his coffee. "Cassie, I know you've been through a lot tonight, but I have some things to discuss with you. Would that be all right?"

"Of course." She set aside her sandwich. Her stomach was too twisted up into knots to even consider eating.

The chief opened a file folder he'd brought in with him. "Mrs. Jennings from the flower shop finally met with the sketch artist. I have a composite of the man who ordered the roses sent to the shelter." He laid a drawing down on the table. "Does he look familiar to you?"

Cassie studied the image. The man had acne-pitted cheeks and hard beady eyes. His age was roughly mid-thirties. Nothing about him was familiar, but he looked like the type of guy Cassie would avoid if she spotted him in the grocery store aisle. A shudder ran down her spine. "I don't know him."

Nathan leaned closer. His arm brushed hers and Cassie welcomed the touch. He must've noticed because he wrapped his arm around her shoulders. "I've never seen him before either, Chief. Have you asked Dwayne? Maybe this guy worked on his construction crew."

Chief Garcia leaned back in his chair. His shoulders sagged. "Dwayne swears he doesn't know him either. Cassie, are you sure you don't recognize him? You haven't seen him around town, perhaps?"

She shook her head. "I'm sorry. I've never seen him before. As much as I hate to say it, he looks like someone I'd remember. And not in a good way." There was a meanness about the man, even in the composite.

Nathan blew out a breath. "Chief, I'd like a copy of this sketch. We've been running down the temporary workers that helped build the new barn on the property, but some names on Dwayne's list were fake. If this man lives in the surrounding area, we can help find him."

Chief Garcia cocked his brow. "And if you locate him, what do you plan to do?"

"Alert the authorities. I'm not a vigilante." Nathan squeezed her shoulder. "I just want Cassie safe."

Kyle and Tucker both nodded. "You have our word, Chief. We'll contact you right away."

The chief nodded. "Okay. I'll take every bit of help I can take. This case has my department stretched thin. We're chasing down every lead, but not making much progress. I still haven't located Jace Hayes."

Cassie stiffened. "About Jace. There's something you should know, Chief." She explained Jace was a smoker and the man who'd attacked her hadn't smelled like cigarettes. "It's a strong possibility Jace isn't my stalker."

"Hold on there. Jace is an experienced criminal with a long rap sheet. I'm sure he's smart enough to have avoided anything that might identify him. Including not smoking before attempting to kidnap you." The chief pointed to the sketch. "Honestly, I wouldn't be surprised to find out this man has been arrested before. He may know Jace, be working with him. I've sent the composite to every law enforcement agency in the state, but so far, no one has identified him."

Cassie's blood ran cold. Nathan had warned her of the same thing after the incident at the shelter. Things were spiraling out of control.

And there was no end in sight.

EIGHTEEN

Morning sunshine streamed across the pasture. Cassie stood in front of the still-smoldering barn. Her eyes were blurry from a lack of sleep no amount of caffeine would erase. The stalker hadn't called or texted again last night, thank goodness, but it didn't make her feel any more at ease. He was out there, planning his next move. She could feel it.

"You can rebuild." Nathan toed a broken board.

She didn't know whether to weep or laugh. Her bank account was running on fumes as it was. But she didn't have the mental energy to think about that now. "We'll figure it out."

Some of her distress must've been evident in her expression because Nathan wrapped his arms around her. She leaned into the touch. Cassie knew it wasn't wise, but she was so tired of being strong. It was lonely.

The fabric of Nathan's shirt was soft under her cheek, his heart-beat strong and steady. Last night's threats seemed a thousand years away within the comfort of his arms. She wanted to stay here forever. But could she? There was so much hurt between them, it felt like an impossible canyon to traverse. Things were such a mess.

Cassie sighed. "What's happening between us?"

"I don't know." Nathan's mouth brushed the top of her head. "I know what I want to have happen."

"Which is?"

He pulled back, gently taking her chin between his thumb and forefinger, lifting her face until she met his gaze. "I love you, Cass. I never stopped. If there's any chance—any chance at all—that you can forgive me, then I will spend the rest of my life proving to you that it wasn't a mistake."

Her heart thundered in her chest. She hadn't expected Nathan to just come right out with the love word. The look in his warm green eyes was intoxicating. She wanted to drown in them.

Cassie's gaze dropped to Nathan's mouth. A part of her was screaming to kiss him. The other, more reasonable part, recognized that would be a huge mistake. The truth was, she hadn't forgiven him. Wasn't sure she could. And no matter how much she cared about Nathan, it wasn't fair to mislead him.

She swallowed hard. "I don't know how I feel. I care about you, Nathan, but I won't make promises I can't keep. I don't know what the future holds. Everything is a confusing mess. And right now, I'm overwhelmed and exhausted."

"I'm sorry. I didn't mean to make this harder on you."

Cassie shook her head. "I'm the one who asked. You told me the truth."

The sound of a vehicle coming up the drive reached her ears. Nathan must've heard it, too, because his head swiveled in that direction even as his muscles tensed. Then he relaxed as Bessie's SUV came into view, bouncing over the ruts in the dirt road. The moment the vehicle stopped, Eric sprang out. He raced toward them.

"Mom wants to take me to visit Grandma, Cassie." Eric's eyes were filled with worry. "Tell her she can't. I have a job to do."

Bessie climbed out of her vehicle. Tucker also exited, his auburn beard shimmering in the sunlight. Cassie waved a greeting. After the attack last night, they'd had a meeting and decided the fewer people on the ranch, the better. Whoever Cassie's stalker was, he wasn't going away. Bessie and Eric would stay with family for the time being. Tucker would act as their bodyguard, keeping them safe until the danger was over.

Cassie hugged Eric. "Don't worry. Your job will be here when you get back. Besides, you love visiting your grandmother. She bakes the best chocolate chip cookies."

He tilted his head. "That's true."

She laughed. "Do me a favor. Bring me some this time."

Eric's smile widened, bunching his cheeks. "Okay." His gaze flickered to the wreckage behind her and he gasped. "Cassie, what happened to the barn?"

"There was a fire last night." She wrapped an arm around his waist and steered him toward Bessie's truck. "But all the horses are just fine. You don't need to worry about anything."

"But where will they sleep?" His voice rose with anxiety.

Cassie pointed to the new barn. "Right there. Isn't it fortunate we have the second barn built and ready to go?"

As the words fell from her lips, she realized just how true they were. Yes, losing the old barn was devastating. But things could be so much worse. Cassie had a place for her horses, and everyone was safe. It was a blessing.

A blessing. It jolted Cassie, and she glanced at the smoldering barn and then the new one. A Biblical verse popped into her head. One of Papa Joe's favorites.

And God is able to bless you abundantly, so that in all things at all times, having all that you need, you will abound in every good work.

Had God been providing for her all this time? Her gaze swept over the ranch, Nathan and Tucker talking, Papa Joe hugging Bessie, and then landed on Eric. Gratefulness swept over her. It was so strong, so deep, Cassie couldn't ignore it.

God, if by chance you're listening, thank you. Thank you.

She focused back on Eric. "Have a good time with your grandmother. She's going to be so happy to see you."

He hugged her one more time, patted Bruiser on the head, and then climbed into the back seat of the truck. Cassie hugged Bessie tightly. "Stay safe."

"You too, hon."

Nathan and Tucker shook hands. Papa Joe also shook hands with the former Army Ranger. "Protect them as if they were your own."

"I will, sir." Tucker's expression was grave. "You have my word. I'll keep them safe."

Minutes later, Cassie waved a last time as Bessie's truck disappeared from sight. A sense of relief washed over her. She would miss Eric and Bessie terribly, but it was far more important they were far away, out of the reach of her stalker.

Papa Joe patted Nathan on the shoulder in a fatherly gesture. "You've got some good friends. Thank you, son, for everything. I don't know what we would've done without your help."

Nathan grinned. "You're no wallflower. I'm pretty sure it was your excellent shooting that saved my skin last night."

They all laughed. It warmed Cassie's heart to see Nathan and Papa Joe together. She knew her grandfather's words had deep meaning for Nathan. Losing his own father at a young age had affected him deeply. When they were dating, Nathan had considered Papa Joe to be a surrogate dad.

Once again, Cassie's muddled feelings came to the surface. Nathan fit with her family. If she was being honest, he fit on her ranch too. His gentle nature and firm hand had earned the trust of every rescue horse on her property. He was also the bravest man Cassie had ever met. He'd put his life on the line for her over and over again, without question or regard for his own well-being.

As if he was following her thoughts, Nathan's gaze collided with hers. It made Cassie's breath hitch. The man was heartbreakingly handsome. His smile was broad, the dimple in his cheek winking. There was so much warmth in his gaze, Cassie was once again tempted to give in to her heart's desire and kiss him senseless.

Papa Joe lifted his hand to shield his gaze from the sun. "Is that Holt coming up the drive?"

Cassie tore her gaze away from Nathan. Sure enough, Holt's pickup truck was heading in their direction. "I called him this morning to ask if he would stop by and look at the horses. I want to make sure the smoke didn't do any damage to their lungs."

Holt parked and climbed out of his truck. His expression was serious as he pulled a medical bag out of the back seat of the extended cab. Cassie moved to intercept him. "Thanks for coming."

"You don't have to thank me, Cassie." He greeted her with a stiff smile that didn't reach his eyes. "Let's see about your animals."

The next hour was spent looking over every horse. Nathan didn't intrude, but he kept a constant presence nearby. Visual range —as he would put it. Cassie felt better with him near. The chances of Holt being her stalker were slim, but the flash of worry she'd had in the coffee shop the last time they met lingered. She couldn't shake it.

As a result, Cassie would've preferred not to have Holt on the property at all, but he was the only veterinarian within a thirty-mile radius. He was also familiar with her horses. They needed to be checked for smoke inhalation. Holt was the only one available to do it.

He peppered her with questions about the attacks against her while conducting exams. She paid attention to his comments. They appeared genuine, which only created more conflict inside Cassie. Her suspicions of Holt weren't based on anything more than a bad feeling. Was she overreaching? Maybe.

And yet...the pinprick of wariness wouldn't leave her.

"Everything looks good." Holt patted Starlight's shoulder before turning to Cassie. "I would take it easy with the horses for the next week. Don't over exert them with training or exercise. Give their lungs a chance to rest after the smoke inhalation."

Relief uncoiled some of the tension in her stomach. Cassie had been anxious about her horses. "Sounds easy enough. Anything I should watch out for while they recover?"

"There's a chance they could develop an upper respiratory infection. If you notice them breathing heavy, coughing excessively, fever, or acting listless, call me."

That would be easy enough. "Okay."

Holt picked up his medical bag, his gaze darting toward Nathan near the fence line before settling back on Cassie. "Walk me to my truck?"

He wanted to speak to her in private. About what? That instinctive uneasiness grew bigger, but Cassie shook it off. Holt had never given her a reason to be afraid of him. Besides, Nathan and Papa Joe were both nearby. She was safe.

Cassie nodded. "Sure."

They fell into step beside each other. An awkward silence descended between them. Finally, Holt cleared his throat. "What's going on between you and Nathan? I've heard rumors he's your ex-fiancé."

The question caught her off-guard, and Cassie mentally berated herself for it. Holt's question was legitimate. They weren't exclusively dating, but they'd been out a couple of times. He'd expressed serious interest in her.

They arrived at Holt's truck and he turned to face her. Cassie licked her lips. "Nathan is my ex-fiancé. He's been staying on the ranch since the first attack, helping to protect me and my family."

"You could've called me."

Holt's jaw tightened. His expression had Cassie taking a step backward. Her mouth suddenly felt dry as dust. It was time to forgo letting him down gently. "I didn't want to. Holt, I'm not interested in you romantically."

107

His eyes turned flat. Terrifyingly flat. "You don't know what you're saying."

"Yes, I do." She jutted up her chin, attempting to fake a confidence she didn't feel.

"Don't do this, Cassie. I asked around. I heard about what Nathan did to you, disappearing without warning on your wedding day. I know guys like him. They like to play women, break their hearts, and then reappear with apologies and promises that they've changed. Do you really think he's going to stick by your side after all of this is over?"

Holt's face grew redder with each word and his voice rose until he was yelling. Cassie took another step away from him. His hatred for Nathan was palpable, a living breathing energy that threatened to engulf her. "You need to leave."

If Holt noticed her fear, or her order, it didn't stop him. He stalked closer. "Nathan is just here to save the day and be a hero. Then he'll leave you high and dry like he did the first time."

A growl came from behind Cassie, and seconds later, Connor, Jason's German shepherd, appeared by her side. Bruiser joined him. The two dogs had taken a liking to each other, practically becoming best friends overnight. Where one was, the other wasn't far behind.

Holt stopped dead in his tracks. Both dogs growled again, baring their teeth.

"I wouldn't move any closer to Cassie, if I were you." Jason's voice carried across the distance. "The dogs are very protective of her."

Cassie glanced over her shoulder to see Jason and Nathan approaching quickly. Both men looked as fierce as the two dogs guarding her. Holt must've seen them, too, because he sneered. "Coming to save the day."

Nathan arrived at Cassie's side, placing a hand on the small of her back. "I believe the lady asked you to leave." His expression grew darker. More dangerous. "Do it."

Holt backed up a step. "When he disappears, I won't be around to pick up the pieces." He opened his truck door and shot Cassie one more angry look. "You've made a terrible mistake."

His vehicle roared to life, and he sped off in a shower of dust. Cassie watched him go, a cold fear settling deep in her bones. "Nathan, we were wrong about Holt. He may be my stalker after all."

NINETEEN

It took most of the afternoon, some manual labor, and a cold shower before Nathan's temper settled back to normal. It'd taken every ounce of his self-control not to physically throw Holt off the property. When he'd seen the little weasel towering over Cassie and screaming in her face.... A few choice words came to mind and none of them were terribly Christian.

He touched the dog tags hidden under his shirt, his fingers rubbing over the cross hanging with them. "God, give me the wisdom to do the right thing and the strength to keep Cassie safe."

The prayer helped center his mindset. He said another for Cassie. It broke Nathan's heart to learn that she was struggling in her relationship with the Lord. But miracles happened every day. He had no doubt Cassie would find her way. She was hurting and in pain. Sometimes, it was easiest to take your anger out on those closest to you—including God. Nathan knew that firsthand. He'd been there.

He released his hold on the cross and left the bedroom, heading for the kitchen. Voices and laughter greeted him. Papa Joe was at the kitchen table, his shotgun propped up on the wall behind him. All three dogs—Gus, Bruiser, and Connor—rested at his feet. Kyle and

Jason, along with Jason's wife, Addison, were helping Cassie with lunch. The four of them joked and teased as if they'd been friends forever.

Jason went to grab a biscuit from a napkin-lined basket. Cassie swatted at the Marine's hand, but her smile made it clear she was playing. "I said to put them on the table, not eat them! Everyone else wants one too."

"Then you shouldn't have made them so tempting." In a smooth move, Jason grabbed a biscuit with one hand and the basket with the other. Under Cassie's glare, he bit into the biscuit and groaned. "They're so good."

"Gimme one of those," Kyle said, reaching for the basket.

Jason spun away and elbowed Kyle in the ribs. "Not a chance."

Addison planted her hands on her hips and whistled. "Have you two lost your minds? We are guests, for heaven's sake. Try to find your manners. The dogs are better behaved than you guys."

Cassie placed a hand over her mouth to smother her laughter as Kyle and Jason both followed Addison's orders. Nathan loved seeing her so happy. He crossed the room to be closer to her, leaning against the counter.

Cassie's eyes were bright with merriment when she whispered to Nathan, "Two tough military men brought down by one sharp-tongued woman."

Nathan chuckled. "Addison's an attorney. Tougher than most. She's used to our horseplay now and knows how to keep us in line."

"I can see that." Cassie touched his arm. "They're wonderful, Nathan. All of them. I'm so glad you have such good friends in your life."

"Something tells me they're your friends now too. And I wouldn't have it any other way."

She beamed, and Nathan's heart did a flip. He couldn't stop himself from planting a kiss on her forehead. Then he grabbed the platter of fried chicken from the counter and headed for the table before he gave in to the temptation to give Cassie more than a chaste peck.

Their relationship was on shaky ground. He needed to remember that. And Nathan would never, ever do anything to pressure Cassie into something she didn't want.

Dinner was an easy affair, full of laughter and stories. Once it was over, however, and the plates were cleared, Nathan leaned forward. "We need to go over what we know so far."

Jason and Kyle nodded. Their expressions grew grim. Addison reached out and touched Cassie's hand, squeezing it lightly in support. Even Papa Joe sat up straighter in his chair. Every single person turned to look at Nathan.

He pulled out a notepad from his back pocket. He'd written some ideas and questions. "Where are we on the drone?"

"Professional grade." Kyle's tone was controlled, but there was a thread of anger running through it. "Rigged for a gun to be mounted on it. Assembling it wouldn't be difficult since there are tutorials showing you how to do it online. It would take limited tech knowledge. Flying the drone well, however, takes skill and practice. Especially at night."

"He was good at it." Nathan replayed the attack in his mind. "He did an excellent job of avoiding my bullets. I wasn't the best shot in the military, but I'm no slouch either. And I've kept up my skills through regular practice. Do we know if Holt or Jace have ever taken a professional drone flying course?"

"Not to our knowledge, but it's something worth digging into more." Kyle frowned. "We're also still working our way through the list Dwayne provided. There are six people we haven't been able to track down. Probably because they gave fake names."

"What about the composite sketch? Where are we on that?"

"Walker is still working on identifying Mr. Roses." Jason rubbed his bristled chin. "No luck yet. And Logan is still tracking Jace

Hayes. He's spoken to Jace's former friends, but no one has seen him for months. Or, at least, that's what they're claiming."

Nathan's shoulders sagged. Every lead they chased down was important, but things weren't moving fast enough. It was frustrating. They needed a break in the case, and soon.

Cassie's phone rang. Nathan stiffened and his gaze shot in her direction.

She glanced at the screen and then shook her head in response to Nathan's silent question and mouthed Leah before answering the call. She got up from the table and went into the living room to speak to her best friend without disturbing them.

"If you want my opinion, Jace Hayes is the man to focus on," Kyle said, bringing the conversation back to the issue at hand. "He's got a long rap sheet and a history with Cassie. Eric too."

Nathan tilted his head. "What do you mean by that?"

"Eric was attacked in the first attempt to grab Cassie, and his horse was trapped in the stall last night. It makes me wonder if the stalker was targeting Eric specifically."

Interesting theory. Nathan turned it over his mind. "It's definitely possible. Except...you should have seen Holt's face today. He was furious about my relationship with Cassie. He threatened her."

Jason rubbed his hand along the scar crisscrossing his cheek. "I agree. That guy is one scary dude. I could easily see him being the stalker. Cassie mentioned that he'd never acted that way with her before."

"Typical abuser behavior." Addison's mouth flattened into a thin line. "He hides his true self because he knows people don't find it acceptable. But then something triggers him and he can't contain his rage."

Nathan arched his brows. Addison was a divorce attorney, specializing in aiding women who'd been in abusive relationships. If she thought Holt was potentially violent, it was something to pay attention to. "Do you think an abuser can control his rage well enough to plan out these attacks on Cassie?"

"Absolutely. There are abusive men who look like respectable husbands and fathers to the outside world. It's only behind closed doors that their real personality comes out."

Before Nathan could ask another follow-up question, Cassie came back into the room. Her brows were drawn together, creating cute little crinkles on her forehead. She set her phone down on the table. "Leah said the shelter received a report that someone abandoned puppies on the ranch next door. She's the only one working tonight and was hoping one of us could check it out."

Nathan shared a glance with Kyle and Jason. The looks on their faces confirmed his own intuition. It sounded like a setup. "Did she say who called the shelter to report the puppies?"

"No." Cassie shrugged. "But that property has been standing empty for a while. There's a house on it that's begging to be torn down. You'd be surprised how many people drop off their unwanted puppies and kittens over there. We get calls at least twice a month. I'm almost sure that's how Muffin ended up in our barn. Someone probably dumped her there when they realized she was pregnant and she walked over to our property."

"I'll check it out." Nathan stood. "Kyle, do you want to come with me? Jason and Addison can stay to keep Cassie and Papa Joe company."

Jason wasn't there only for good conversation, but Nathan didn't feel the need to drive home the danger Cassie was in. The former Marine winked and then rubbed his stomach. "Perfect. I get dibs on dessert."

Addison laughed. "No, you don't. We'll wait until everyone gets back."

Jason snagged her hand and pulled her closer for a kiss. It was a simple gesture but so full of love and passion that it seemed far more intimate. Nathan's gaze skipped away from the couple and landed on

Cassie. There had been a time their relationship was like Jason and Addison's. Could they ever get that back?

Cassie's cheeks turned a pretty pink under the weight of his gaze. She cleared her throat, sliding past Nathan to the laundry room. "I'll get the pet carriers."

Fifteen minutes later, Nathan steered his truck down the back road linking the two properties together. His headlights illuminated a ramshackle farmhouse. Part of the roof had caved in. Weeds grew wild and free where the porch used to be and one lingering shutter tilted precariously on a single nail.

Nathan parked but didn't kill his headlights. He and Kyle got out of the car. Both drew their weapons.

"Thanks for bringing me to a creepy haunted house." Kyle craned his head. "It's not even Halloween."

Nathan shot him a glance. "Don't be a chicken."

"Watch who you call chicken. I'm the dude guarding your six."

Wind rustled through the trees. The hair on the back of Nathan's neck stood on end. Despite his teasing, he was grateful to have Kyle watching his back. Something about this didn't feel right. And Nathan had learned a long time ago to always listen to his instincts. "Let's get this over with."

They circled around the back of the house. Nathan kept his ears peeled for any noise, including the yip of a puppy. Broken beer bottles and fast food wrappers littered the cement stoop. The screen door was hanging from one hinge, the back door left wide open. A glimmer snagged Nathan's attention. He swung his gun in that direction.

The beam of his headlights shone through the house. An odd shape was inside. Nathan couldn't make out what it was. "Kyle, we're going in."

"Lead the way, cousin."

Nathan pulled the screen door opened. It screeched in protest, grating against his over sensitized nerves. Leading with his gun, he entered the room, Kyle right behind him. They swung left and right before focusing on the object in the center of the house. Nathan inhaled sharply.

It was Chief Garcia. He was bound to a chair with duct tape. Blood pooled from his body onto the floor from a gunshot wound. The headlights caught on the badge pinned to his chest. That'd been the glimmer Nathan saw.

He bolted forward. Pressing two fingers to the other man's throat, Nathan checked for a pulse and was relieved to find one. It was weak, but it was there. "We need paramedics. He's alive."

Kyle yanked out his cell phone while Nathan ripped off his shirt and used it to staunch the wound. The sound of Kyle speaking to dispatch became background noise. Nathan's gaze darted around the dimly lit room. His heart dropped to his chest and then slammed right back up into his throat.

Written on the wall, in blood, was a message.

I warned you, sugar plum. No one can come between us.

TWENTY

The emergency room waiting area was bustling with activity. A steady stream of ambulances arrived and left while more people gathered on the hard plastic chairs. Nathan paced along the window overlooking the parking lot. His gaze swept the area, watching for any sign of the stalker.

No, the attempted murderer. Chief Garcia was in surgery, but he'd lost a lot of blood before they got to the hospital. Nathan had been in enough combat to know the chief's odds weren't good.

Cassie sat quietly nearby, comforting Chief Garcia's wife. The woman was beside herself. She couldn't stop crying. It was eating Nathan up inside and his pacing increased. He probably resembled a caged tiger. It's how he felt. He'd already said half a dozen prayers while riding in the ambulance and again in the waiting room. There was nothing left to do but wait.

Someone's gaze was on him. Nathan turned and caught sight of a couple staring in his direction. He looked down and realized he was covered in blood. Chief Garcia's blood. He'd washed his hands, but the undershirt was destroyed. At this rate, he wouldn't have any clothes left to wear soon.

"Here." Kyle took off his button-down and handed it to Nathan.

"Thanks." Nathan quickly pulled his cousin's shirt on and did up the buttons. His gaze drifted back to the window and the parking lot beyond. "Do you think this was a trick to get Cassie here?"

"It's possible. We can't discount anything."

Nathan nodded. His cousin's warning supported his own instincts. The stakes were getting higher and higher. Cassie wasn't the only one in danger. There was no telling how many people her stalker was willing to hurt. Nathan wanted him stopped. Now.

A set of men crossing the parking lot snagged Nathan's attention. They didn't wear police uniforms, but they walked like cops. Cowboy hats, boots, and khakis acted like a uniform. The men grew closer and Nathan instantly recognized one of them. Texas Ranger Grady West. Jason must've phoned his buddy, just as he promised.

The hospital doors swished open and Grady made a beeline for Nathan. "You causing trouble again? What happened, Nathan? Getting shot once didn't scare you away from hunting down criminals."

Grady was referring to the bullet wound Nathan had gotten while protecting Jason's wife, Addison. Nathan arched his brows. "I can't leave all the fun to you guys."

The Texas Ranger laughed, but there was genuine worry in Grady's eyes. He shook Nathan's hand warmly before doing the same with Kyle. Then he jutted a thumb toward his colleague. "This is Texas Ranger Weston Donovan. He's assisting me on the case."

The men shook hands and exchanged pleasantries. Nathan had been one of the largest men in his Green Beret unit, but Weston outsized him by nearly fifty pounds. The man was a moving tank.

Cassie joined the group, leaving Chief Garcia's wife with an officer from the police department to comfort her. Another round of introductions were made.

Nathan positioned himself between Cassie and the window. Just in case. The scent of her shampoo drifted across his nose and he breathed it in. Some of the tension in his muscles relaxed. She was okay, safe, here with him.

He intended to keep it that way.

"I've visited the crime scene and spoken to several members of Chief Garcia's staff," Grady said. "The chief was on patrol when a call came in claiming that some kids were fooling around at the abandoned house. Chief Garcia volunteered to stop by and break up the party since it was on his way home. There seems to be a breakdown in communication after that. Dispatch thought the chief had simply gone home after chasing away the kids without radioing in."

"Mrs. Garcia mentioned her husband had a bad habit of doing that." Cassie blew out a breath. "And she thought he was still at work. No one was looking for him or realized he was in trouble."

"That's the consensus. I also spoke to Leah Gray at the shelter. She didn't recognize the person who called to report the puppies, but it was a male voice. Faint Texas or Southern accent. She couldn't identify any noises in the background or anything else we could use to further identify the person."

Nathan rocked back on his heels. Most of Knoxville had a Texas or Southern accent. That didn't help narrow things down at all. "Have you checked to see where Holt Adler was earlier this evening?"

"I did." Weston's voice was thick, like molasses. "Holt claims he was home. Alone. Neighbors confirmed his truck was in the driveway of his house from 6:30 onward."

That didn't rule Holt out, but it gave Nathan pause. The abandoned property was a good five miles from Holt's residence. He could've walked or even run it, but that was unlikely. His house was near the center of town. A neighbor would've spotted him on the road.

"What about Jace Hayes?" Kyle asked.

"Still in the wind." Grady removed his cowboy hat and scratched his forehead. "We've got every officer in the state looking for him.

Along with the mystery man in the composite sketch. So far, nothing."

"Garcia family," a man in scrubs announced.

Nathan held his breath as Mrs. Garcia waved and stood up. The officer at her side kept his hand on her elbow. Cassie's shoulders grew stiffer with every step the doctor took. She reached back and grabbed Nathan's hand. He intertwined their fingers.

The doctor's gaze swept around the group before settling on the chief's wife. "Your husband is out of surgery, ma'am, and in the ICU. The bullet did a lot of damage to his internal organs and it's going to be touch-and-go for a while, but he has an excellent shot at making a full recovery." He paused. "Can you tell me who found your husband?"

"These men." Mrs. Garcia pointed to Nathan and Kyle.

The doctor nodded in their direction. "The paramedics said you provided top-notch first aid. Your quick actions saved Chief Garcia's life and gave him a fighting chance."

Cassie squeezed Nathan's hand, tears shimmering in her eyes. Mrs. Garcia came and embraced him and then Kyle. The praise and gratitude from Chief Garcia's wife was kind, but it felt hollow. Nathan didn't feel like a hero. Not while the man who'd shot Chief Garcia was still running the streets, capable of hurting others. He wouldn't rest until the criminal was sitting in a prison cell.

Mrs. Garcia left with the doctor to see her husband. Nathan sent up another prayer, asking God to watch over the entire Garcia family. They would need a lot of patience in the coming weeks and months. The road to recovery was a long one. That was something Nathan could attest to.

"I don't think there is anything more you guys can do tonight." Grady clapped Nathan on the shoulder. "Go home and get some much needed rest. I'll call you in the morning with an update."

Nathan doubted he'd get a wink of sleep, but Cassie looked dead on her feet. The adrenaline had faded from her system and she was crashing. No wonder. She'd been through a lot in the last couple of days. They all said their goodbyes and headed for the exit.

The night air cooled Nathan's skin as he scanned the parking lot once more. He snagged Cassie's hand, interlocking their fingers together again, and tugging her closer to him. The florescent lights cast large beams on the concrete, but there were shadows big enough to hide a person. Too many of them. "Where did you park, Kyle?"

"Second row. Third on the right."

It wasn't too far. Nathan let his cousin lead the way, keeping his gaze sharp and his ears pricked for any noise. Kyle's black 4x4 came into view. The vehicle chirped as the locks disengaged.

A scraping sound came from between two cars. Nathan shifted his position, catching sight of a man hidden a few yards away. Their gazes locked. Dark messy hair, tattoos on his neck, thin lips. Nathan's chest tightened as recognition smacked him across the face.

Jace Hayes.

"Freeze! Don't move!" Nathan shoved Cassie toward Kyle and pulled his handgun with one smooth motion. There was no time to explain, but his cousin wouldn't need one. He'd protect Cassie.

Jace bolted.

Nathan sprinted after him.

TWENTY-ONE

Jace escaped.

Cassie parted the curtains and looked out at the pasture. A brilliant sunset blaze across the sky, painting the world in golden hues. Twilight was just around the corner. And then it would be evening.

It was silly to be afraid of the darkness—her stalker had attacked in broad daylight without compunction—but the night scared Cassie most. The property was over 100 acres. It was impossible for her self-appointed bodyguards to be everywhere at once. It felt like she was waiting...waiting for him to make his next move. Last night, he'd shot Chief Garcia. What would come next?

Cassie's cell phone rang, and she jumped. Sick dread churned in her belly as she crossed the room to her nightstand. Eric's name flashed across the screen. She breathed out a sigh of relief and answered. "Hey, you."

"Cassie, you'll never believe it." Eric's sweet voice was filled with excitement. "I rode a bicycle today! Tucker taught me how."

His exuberance brought a smile to her face. It was a huge accomplishment for him. Eric was an outstanding horse rider, but he'd never managed to figure out a bicycle. She sat on the bed. "I'm so proud of you. Did your mom take photos?"

"Yep, and video. She's going to send them to you."

"I can't wait to see it." Muffin twined between her legs and she scratched the cat behind her ears. The poor thing hadn't been enthusiastic about being trapped in Cassie's bedroom, but she was warming up to the idea. Her kittens were resting inside their basket. They looked like a misshaped bundle of fur.

"I miss you, Cassie. Are the horses okay? How is Casper?"

"He's fine. Everyone here is doing great." It was a fib. Okay, a big one. But Eric's anxiety would go through the roof if he knew about the dangerous situations happening on the ranch. There was no need to upset him. "Are you having a good time with your grandmother?"

"Yep. I told her what you said about the chocolate chip cookies. She promised we could make some to bring to you." Eric was quiet for a moment. "How long do I have to stay away? I like being at home. Mom won't tell me when the vacation will be over."

Cassie didn't have an answer for him, and it broke her heart. Eric was used to his own routine. It wasn't easy for him to adjust to a new place, even if it was familiar. She wanted to reach inside the phone and give him a hug. "I know it's hard, but think about the great thing you did today. Riding a bicycle. It's amazing. You should ask Tucker what else he can show you."

"That's a good idea. I'm going to do that right now. Bye, Cassie."

He hung up. Cassie smiled and scratched Muffin's ears, listening to the rumble of her purr. "I may convince you to become a house cat yet." She sighed. "I wish all my problems could be solved so easily."

A meow came from the basket and Muffin abandoned Cassie to check on her kittens. She was a good momma.

Cassie slipped from the bedroom, being careful to close the door behind her. Bruiser was sleeping in the hall. He greeted her with several sniffs. She patted his head. "I know, I know. There's a cat in my room and it's driving you crazy. Come on, I'll give you a doggie treat."

Bruiser trotted ahead of her to the living room. Papa Joe was asleep in the recliner, his trusty shotgun by his side. A wave of tenderness swept over Cassie. She grabbed the blanket from the back of the couch and covered her grandfather with it. Then she went into the kitchen.

Nathan was sitting at the table. He was working on his laptop, a cup of coffee at his elbow, and a frown on his handsome face. His hair was damp from a recent shower, but he hadn't shaved. Dark bristles coated his jaw, giving him a rugged appearance. It appealed to her. Everything about the man appealed to her.

Without even meaning to, Cassie's feet drew her closer. She placed a hand on his shoulder. "Everything okay?"

Nathan glanced up, warmth flooding his expression. He pushed out the chair closest to him. "Sit down. There have been some developments."

"Let me give Bruiser a treat first." The dog was waiting patiently by the pantry door. Cassie quickly fed him a doggie bone. It was gone in one bite. "Did you even taste that?"

Bruiser tilted his head one way and then the other, as if trying to understand what she was saying. Cassie planted a kiss on his broad forehead. "Such a good boy."

"You're spoiling that dog," Nathan said, without looking up from his computer screen.

"I'm starting to think you're jealous."

He flashed a broad grin at her flirty comment. That irresistible dimple in his cheek winked. "Oh, there's no question about that. Bruiser drools, doesn't bathe daily, and still, he gets special treats and a pat on the head."

Cassie laughed, crossed to the table, and patted Nathan on the head. "Should I give you a doggie treat too?"

He snagged her hand, planting a kiss on the inside of her palm.

Her breath hitched. Nathan's lips were warm and the bristles around his mouth created a delicious sensation against her skin. Desire pooled in her belly, potent and heady. It froze her in place. She couldn't move. Not toward him or away.

It was their relationship in a nutshell. And Cassie didn't know how to navigate it.

Nathan must've sensed their teasing went too far. He released her hand. "Ready to talk business?"

Her legs were like jelly. How did he do that? Switch gears so quickly? Maybe everything she was feeling, he didn't. Or maybe not as strongly. Her thoughts were jumbled and not making much sense. Nathan had that effect on her.

She sank into the kitchen chair and ran her hands through her hair, tucking a few unruly strands behind her ear. "Hit me with it."

"Walker finally identified the man from the flower shop composite sketch." Nathan tapped on his mouse pad and then turned the laptop screen toward Cassie. "His name is Maddox Brown. Career criminal. Burglary, bad checks, theft, and drugs. A couple of assaults, but they were drug related."

She stared at Maddox. The photograph had been taken from an arrest last year. It seemed impossible, but he was even meaner looking in a picture than he'd been in the composite sketch. A shudder rippled down her spine. "I've never met this man before in my life. Do you think Chief Garcia was right and the real stalker hired him to send the flowers?"

"It's the prevailing theory at the moment. Walker has forwarded all the information he has to Grady and Weston. The rangers have every law enforcement officer in the state looking for Maddox. He so much as sneezes and they'll find him."

Cassie sat back in her chair. Her cell phone, tucked in her back pocket, poked her. She removed it, setting it on the table. "Does he have any connection to Jace? They were both in prison."

"We're still checking, but at the moment, we don't have anything linking the two men together. They run in different criminal circles and were housed in different prisons. Having said that, we're still in the preliminary stages. Guys like Jace and Maddox tend to find one another."

Cassie drummed her nails on the table. "I can't make heads or tails of this. If Jace is my stalker, why on earth run away last night? I mean, if he shot Chief Garcia to get my attention, or to get me to the hospital, then why not attack?"

"Maybe he wasn't counting on Kyle. Until recently, I've been the only one guarding you."

She supposed that was possible. "I keep thinking about Jace's smoking. I know it's a silly thing to cling to, but I'm certain the man who attacked me didn't smell like cigarettes at all. And it's not an easy scent to get rid of. Even if you wash your clothes, it clings to every fabric you own, like the seats in your car."

"I know what you're saying, Cass, but I think Chief Garcia was right about this too. Jace is smart enough to have eliminated anything that could help identify him. I mean, he wore a ski mask to attack you too. He wasn't taking any risks." Nathan pushed away his computer. "Logan found several of Jace's ex-girlfriends. He's got a violent temper. Beat one woman bad enough to put her in the hospital for a week."

"Sweet mercy. Did she press charges?"

"No. In fact, she refused to tell the police who'd hurt her because, and I quote, they can't protect me. The only reason Logan convinced her to talk to him was because he explained about you." Nathan's gaze hardened. "According to the ex-girlfriend, Jace talked about you a lot. Called you his first love."

Bile rose in Cassie's throat. Her hands trembled, and she clenched them together to keep it from Nathan. But he caught it anyway.

"I'm sorry. I shouldn't have—"

"No. You need to tell me everything." She locked gazes with him. "I can handle it, Nathan. I'm stronger than you think."

Her words came out harsher than she intended. Nathan winced. A pang of regret followed, but Cassie didn't take it back. He'd blown up their relationship by refusing to believe that she could handle his career as a Green Beret. The last thing she wanted was for Nathan to make any more decisions for her.

Cassie's cell phone rang. The sick feeling in her stomach intensified when she saw the number was private. Her stalker.

She needed to answer. Every call provided a new opportunity for the police to find him. Cassie forced herself to pick up the phone, hit record on the app, and answer the call. "What?"

"Now, now, sugar plum. There's no need to be so rude."

Her hand tightened on the phone. She was sick of this. His toying calls. His attacks. Her fear. Rage unlike anything she'd ever known flooded over her. "You shot a man. That tends to make me testy."

"It was a message, one that clearly hasn't gotten through to you yet. Why is Nathan still there? I'm running out of patience, Cassie. I love you, but I won't tolerate betrayal. Don't keep pushing me. You'll be sorry."

He hung up before she could say anything more. Cassie's gaze lifted to meet Nathan's. "He's done something. Call everyone. We need to make sure they're safe."

TWENTY-TWO

It took over an hour to discover Starlight was missing.

Nathan gripped the steering wheel of the ranch pickup truck as it bounced over a deep rut on the dirt road cutting across the property. Cassie sat in the passenger seat beside him. Her complexion was pale, and she was chewing on her bottom lip so hard it was a wonder she didn't bite right through it. Nathan would've preferred she stay back at the house with Kyle as a bodyguard. Unfortunately, nothing short of tying her to a chair would've prevented Cassie from joining in the search for her beloved horse.

If she was going to be exposed, it was better for her to be with him.

Nathan navigated the truck into the woods. Darkness pressed all around them as the moon disappeared behind a canopy of tree branches. The headlights—on the brightest setting—illuminated the road and nearby bushes. Still, the overgrowth was thick with leaves and flowers this time of year. He peered into the shadows on either side of the road, alert for any sign of an attack. The windows of the truck were also cocked open, making it easier to listen for Starlight.

"I should've bought a lock for the new barn doors." Cassie balled her hands into fists. "How could I have been so stupid? Especially after the old barn burned down."

"You've had a few things on your mind." Nathan never took his eyes from the windshield. "I didn't think of it either. My mistake. I thought having men patrolling the property would be enough of a deterrent."

He'd underestimated the stalker. Again. The criminal had literally waltzed onto the property and removed a horse from the barn under the cover of night. Frustration and anger mingled with worry for Starlight's safety. The emotions churned Nathan's stomach and threatened to distract him. He tamped them down, putting all his focus on the mission. Finding Cassie's horse and the criminal who took him.

A tree branch scraped down the side of the truck and Nathan winced. "How many people could've taken Starlight from the barn?"

"Not that many. He's rehabilitated, but that doesn't mean Starlight trusts everyone. He's still wary of most people."

"So Jace couldn't have taken him, for example?"

Cassie shook her head. "No, I don't think so. Not unless he has extensive education in horse training, which I find hard to believe considering his drug abuse and prison time." She was quiet for a long moment. "Holt could've. Starlight knows him well since he's our veterinarian."

Nathan's hands tightened even more on the steering wheel. He darted a glance toward Cassie before focusing back on the dirt road. "That's what you were alluding to earlier in the kitchen. You don't think Jace is behind this. You think it's Holt."

She rubbed a hand over her face. "I don't know what to think. But if you're asking about my gut instinct...then yes. The way Holt flipped on me yesterday was scary. I've never seen him act like that before. If he can hide that part of himself so well, it leaves me wondering what else he's capable of."

Cassie's feelings mirrored Addison's warning from the other day.

Had Nathan been too rash in narrowing his focus to Jace? It was possible. But if Jace wasn't stalking Cassie, then why on earth had he been watching them from the hospital parking lot? And how did Maddox Brown, aka Mr. Roses, fit into the equation? Nothing about this made sense.

"Take the fork toward the family cemetery." Cassie pointed to the left.

"Why?"

"Gut instinct." Her voice was hard. "My stalker likes to be dramatic."

Nathan did as she instructed and the sound of the river grew louder. His headlights flashed across the ancient oak tree and weathered tombstones. For half a heartbeat, he thought about his own mother's grave. Then he quickly shoved the thought aside. Opening that particular suitcase of emotions wouldn't help. Instead, he focused on navigating the truck around a huge dip in the road.

"Do you hear that?" Cassie's hand shot out, grabbing Nathan's arm, even as she cranked down her window. "Nathan, hit the brakes for a second."

He did as she asked, his gaze darting around the open field. This was the worst place to stop. It left them exposed.

A high-pitched whinny cut through the night air.

Starlight.

The horse was in distress, and based on the direction of the sound, he was near the river. Nathan gunned the engine, steering the truck back into the trees. His heart rate picked up speed. He grabbed his gun from the center console and flicked off the safety. They were walking into a trap. He could feel it.

Cassie pulled her own weapon from its holster. Wind from the open window blew her hair around her face. Another terrified whinny came from Starlight, sending Nathan's worry into overdrive. A thousand possibilities flashed in his mind, one more gruesome than the next. He pushed the truck's gas pedal down. They bounced over a rut and his head hit the roof. Nathan barely felt it.

They rounded a curve in the road and the river came into view. Nathan's gut clenched as he slammed on the brakes. His headlights illuminated the terrifying scene in front of him.

Starlight was standing in the center of the river. Water rushed around his legs, the level high enough to scrape across his belly. His eyes were wide with terror. A noose was tied around the horse's neck, the other end of the rope tied to the overhead branch of a tree. Every effort Starlight made to free himself from the river would tighten the noose. He was trapped.

There was only one way to get him out safely. Someone had to wade into the river and lift the noose off.

Nathan shoved the truck into park but didn't kill the engine. "Cassie, roll up your window and get in the driver's seat. Once I exit, lock the doors behind me."

"I'll go, Nathan." She unhooked her belt. "Starlight knows me—"

"I need you to watch my back." He met her gaze for half a heart-beat. His beautiful, stubborn Cassie. She was fearless when it came to protecting her animals, and the stalker was counting on that. "Stay here and blare the horn if you spot danger."

Nathan didn't give her a chance to respond. Instead, he threw the rusted pickup truck door open and exited the vehicle. He heard the lock snick shut behind him. Starlight tossed his head, letting out another frightened whinny. There was no time to waste. It was a miracle the horse hadn't already hung himself trying to escape the river.

Nathan removed his boots and left them on the bank. The frigid water stole his breath. He kept a tight hold on his handgun, his gaze sweeping the area, but it was little use. The killer could be anywhere. Nathan had to count on Cassie to be his eyes. She wouldn't let him down.

His foot hit a slippery rock on the river bottom. Nathan stumbled, nearly submerging himself in the water. Dangerous. The current was strong enough to sweep him downstream, and while he was a good swimmer, there was still a chance he could drown.

Nathan righted himself and kept going. "I'm coming, Starlight. Just hold on."

His feet grew numb from the cold water. The weight of his soaked jeans slowed him down. He kept talking in a calm voice, working his way to the middle of the river.

There was a small risk Starlight would panic when Nathan approached. The horse was terrified. The only saving grace was that Nathan was upwind from Starlight. Hopefully, he would catch Nathan's scent, hear his voice, and recognize him as a friend.

He kept his gun in one hand and extended the other, reaching for Starlight's halter. The horse nickered in greeting. "Yes, that's it, boy. It's me."

Fighting the current, Nathan drew himself alongside the horse. He paused. There was no way to keep a proper hold on his gun while freeing Starlight. Every cell in Nathan's body was screaming that he was in danger, that this was a trap of some kind. But there was no choice. He had to save Cassie's horse.

He re-engaged the safety on his weapon, moved it to his left hand, and wrapped two fingers around the trigger guard. He clasped Starlight's halter using his primary fingers. Then he reached for the noose around the horse's neck with his right hand.

The truck horn blared. Nathan's gaze shot to the truck. The headlights blinded his view of Cassie inside, but his ears picked up on the danger she was alerting him to.

The whine of an approaching drone.

TWENTY-THREE

Not again.

Cassie spun around in the driver's seat, craning her head to look at the dark sky. Not that she would be able to see the drone easily. But the whine of its propellers grew louder with each slam of her heartbeat. Her gaze shot back to Nathan. He was desperately attempting to remove the noose from Starlight's neck, but it was a slow process, since the rope was so tightly wound.

Exactly as the killer had planned.

He was going to shoot Nathan and Starlight right in front of Cassie as punishment for disobeying him. Well, she wasn't going to sit in the truck and watch it happen. Her fingers fumbled with the lock on the door. Then she shoved the heavy truck door open.

A shot fired. Cassie screamed at the sudden sound. Her heart ricocheted against her rib cage as Nathan disappeared under the water. Starlight whinnied in fear.

No, no, no. God, please, no!

She started running toward the river when Nathan popped up on the other side of the horse. Water streamed from his face and body. No blood. He hadn't been hit. Air whooshed from Cassie's lungs as she released the breath she'd been holding. Nathan immediately began tugging on the rope again. He was alive. Unhurt.

Nothing was going to get to him. Not on her watch.

The drone whirred, readying to aim again. Cassie lifted her handgun and fired. Then fired again. Anger pumped through her veins, narrowing her focus to the flying object in the sky. She wasn't the best shot, but one of her bullets got close enough to count. The drone operator hit reverse.

She never took her gaze off it. Cassie was afraid it would fade into the night and make another sneak attack again. It buzzed through the air.

Whenever it lowered in an attempt to attack, Cassie took aim and fired. She counted her bullets. One more and she would be out of ammunition. She didn't have an extra clip on her. It was in the truck. She mentally berated herself for not remembering to grab it.

The drone spun toward her. Cassie ducked. A bullet slammed into the truck's windshield behind her. The glass shattered. She raised her weapon and fired in retaliation. This time her bullet must've clipped one of the propellers because the drone tilted haphazardly but didn't go down.

"Cassie!" Nathan's shout was panicked. He'd gotten Starlight free and was riding the horse out of the river. The drone spun and took a shot at the pair, but the bullet went wild.

Then they hit solid ground, much to Cassie's relief. Again, the drone fired and missed. How many bullets did it have? Starlight's hooves pounded against the grass as the horse picked up speed. He was heading straight for her. Nathan leaned over the side of the horse, extending his arm.

Cassie grabbed it and Nathan lifted her onto Starlight's back without missing a step. She wrapped her arms around his waist as he urged the horse to move faster. Starlight needed little encouragement. He flew into the cover of the trees as the drone fired one last time.

The bullet whizzed past, close enough Cassie could feel the heat of it, and then they were enveloped in the forest.

Wind tousled the strands of her hair as the sound of the river faded. Nathan's clothes were soaked, but the warmth of his skin bled through. She pressed her cheek to his back. She didn't care if she got wet.

He could have died. He could have died.

The phrase played over and over again in Cassie's head like a bad record. She hugged Nathan tighter, unable to get close enough to stop the horrible what-ifs from flashing in her mind. She didn't know how to process it all. Cassie only recognized that it terrified her to think of losing Nathan. Bone-deep terror, both uncontrollable and illogical.

Muscles rippled under her palms as Nathan navigated Starlight home. Her body trembled and then shook as the adrenaline rush from the last few hours slipped from her body. She closed her eyes and held on.

Cassie was still shaking when they slipped into the barn. Starlight was breathing heavy, the exercise overexerting his smoke-damaged lungs. Somewhere inside her, Cassie mentally recognized that fact, but it felt like there was a filter on her brain. She was here, but not really. Numb.

Nathan dismounted. He gently tugged her from the horse's back but didn't set Cassie on her feet. Instead, he carried her to a nearby chair. He set her down as if she was more precious than spun glass and then wrapped a blanket around her shoulders. She couldn't stop shaking. Her teeth chattered.

Nathan crouched down next to her. "Cassie, look at me."

She lifted her gaze to meet his. His hair stuck out in every direction, his T-shirt was plastered to his skin, and his eyes...oh, they stole what little breath she was able to pull into her lungs. In their depths, fear mingled with concern. And there was love. Deep, deep love.

Cassie lifted a trembling hand to his cheek. The bristles along his jaw pricked her skin.

This man...this brave man. He'd risked his life to save her horse. Nathan didn't fire off one shot. He had a gun, but didn't take time away from freeing Starlight to save himself. It twisted her insides.

Nathan scanned her face. "You need an ambulance. I'll call one."

"No." The word came out sharp, despite the quakes still running through her.

"Cassie, you're in shock—"

She kissed him. Without thinking, without hesitation, she gave into the only feeling cutting through the numbness. Love. She loved him. There was no escaping it, no denying it. It was like the sunshine or gravity. A proven fact.

Nathan rose, pulling Cassie up with him, wrapping his arms around her. The blanket fell from her shoulders. She didn't need it. His mouth skated across hers, igniting the constant flame of desire running between them. Heat blazed through her. She cupped the back of his head with her hand, demanding he deepen the kiss, until they were both breathless with passion.

How long they shared the moment, she didn't know. A minute. Ten. Thirty. It didn't matter. She was lost in him. Nathan was the only man who could make her feel this way. There was no one else. There never had been.

And there never would be.

The thought brought Cassie back to her senses. She pulled away, heart thundering against her rib cage, as the reality of what she'd done slammed into her with the force of a runaway horse. Regret, swift and fierce, knifed through her. No, she couldn't do this. There was no clear path for them. Passion and love had never been the problem.

Trust. That was the problem. Nathan had left her once, and deep down, Cassie knew he would do it again. It was only a matter of time.

She was someone people threw away.

Nathan blinked, caught off-guard by her sudden retreat. The haze cleared from his vision as his gaze skimmed over her expression.

Her face must've said it all, because he immediately released her. Hurt flickered across his face before he could smooth it away.

But she still saw it. A lump formed in the back of Cassie's throat, and she couldn't manage to speak past it. She'd never been good at voicing her fears. Or sharing her feelings.

"It's okay, Cass." Nathan's gaze skittered away from hers. "You don't need to apologize or explain. I understand. We got caught up in a moment."

Those words cut through her heart with the precision of a scalpel. It was so painful she placed a hand on her chest, almost expecting to discover she was bleeding. The kiss had meant everything to her. *Everything.* Which is what made it so utterly terrifying.

Nathan bent and retrieved the blanket from the ground. He gently—ever so gently—wrapped it around Cassie's shoulders. "I'll see to Starlight. Sit."

She sank into the chair, her legs too wobbly to hold her up any longer.

Nathan turned away, never once meeting her gaze.

TWENTY-FOUR

Nathan's kiss lingered on Cassie's lips all night and into the morning. She had a host of problems on her plate—namely a maniac trying to kidnap her—but her mind kept drifting back to the handsome soldier living in her house.

"Earth to Cassie." Leah waved a hand in front of Cassie's face. "I've been talking for the last three minutes and I don't think you've heard one word."

She hadn't. A blush rose in her cheeks. Leah had come over first thing in the morning with a comedy movie and chocolate. It didn't matter that it was barely 10 a.m. They'd downed most of the giant-sized bag of candy bars sitting on the floor between them. The movie was still playing, but it'd been muted half an hour ago as the two women chatted about everything and anything other than the threats.

Muffin rubbed her cheek against Cassie's arm. She absently stroked the tabby. "I'm sorry. Start the story again. I'm listening."

Her friend shot her a sympathetic look. "Never mind. I can tell you another time." Leah's expression grew serious. "Do you want to talk about what's troubling you or should I amuse you with another witty story? A shorter one this time."

Her last comment eeked a smile out of Cassie, which made Leah grin. She adjusted her thick-rimmed glasses and then waved her hand in a forward motion. "Come on. Out with it."

"It's Nathan. We...kissed." Her stomach clenched. "And I'm in love with him."

Leah nodded, a pensive look on her face, and tucked an unruly curl behind her ear. "I figured as much. And?"

"What do you mean, and?" Cassie's voice rose in pitch, and then she realized the words had nearly come out as a shout. She glanced at her closed bedroom door. Nathan wasn't lurking behind it, but the walls in the old house were thin and she didn't want him overhearing this conversation. "Things are a colossal mess. Nathan and I can't get back together. Kissing him was a huge mistake."

"I'm not sure I understand. Back up one step. Why can't you and Nathan get back together?"

Cassie scratched behind Muffin's ears. The cat's purring increased. Why had she started this conversation? It was going to take her down a direction Cassie wasn't sure she wanted to go. Then again, maybe it was time to voice her fears. Keeping them inside wasn't helping.

Cassie licked her lips. "He left me. He tried to explain it was his fault, that it had nothing to do with me, but..."

Leah reached out and touched Cassie's leg. "You think he's lying."

Silly, ridiculous tears flooded her eyes. Her chin trembled. "I don't think he's lying on purpose. Nathan believes what he's saying, but I know it's not the truth. There's something wrong with me." A lone tear floated down her cheek, and she angrily swiped it away. "People abandon me. It started with my mother and continued with Nathan. Papa Joe won't eat right, no matter what I say, because he's ready to leave me too. Even God has left me."

Saying the words out loud ripped off the bandages Cassie had applied to cover up her pain. She choked on a sob. Leah came to sit beside her and didn't hesitate to wrap her arms around her in a comforting embrace. "No, Cass. You have it all wrong."

Cassie couldn't speak, the sobs threatening to sever the last ounce of self-control she had. She knew this would happen. Talking about it had been a terrible mistake. No one could make this better. In a few moments, she was going to be curled up on her bedroom floor, crying her eyes out.

"God has never left you." Leah released Cassie to pull several tissues from the bedside table. She handed them over. "He will never leave you."

Her friend's words struck a chord. Hadn't Cassie seen evidence of God working in her life? Felt a pull toward prayer she'd even given in to every now and again. Most noticeably yesterday when she'd thought Nathan was shot. She sucked in a shuddering breath. "Even if that's true, that doesn't change the rest."

"Maybe, but I would argue, you're looking at things through the wrong lens."

Cassie swiped at her tears. "I don't understand."

"Let's start with your mom." Leah stroked one of Muffin's kittens that had tumbled into her lap. A few more tumbled around on the carpet nearby. "I know it hurt when she left you, but she wasn't capable of being a good mother. Coming to live here changed your life for the better. Papa Joe's too. He was heartbroken after losing his wife, and then you showed up...Cass, you were a miracle for him. A grandchild he never knew he had."

The truth of Leah's words was like a sweet summer rain on the raging pain inside Cassie. But it wouldn't be that easy to snuff out what she'd been believing for her whole life.

"Papa Joe doesn't eat bacon because he's on a mission to leave you." Leah smiled gently. "He does it because he's a stubborn man who doesn't like to be told what to do." She arched her brows. "That trait runs in the family."

Cassie burst out laughing. She couldn't deny it. She was terribly stubborn. "And Nathan?"

"He made a mistake. A terrible one, yes, but Nathan did it with a misguided notion of protecting you."

Leah was right. Nathan hadn't been malicious when he left Cassie at the altar. He'd felt trapped between his love for her and his dream of becoming a Green Beret. Their conversation from the other night had rolled around in her head for days. And if Cassie was truly honest with herself, there'd been a lot of truth in Nathan's fears. She would've walked through fire to be with him, but his career would've separated them. Secret missions, never knowing if he would come home at night, disappearing from places without notice...it would've hurt her.

Cassie hadn't been honest about that. It's something they could've gotten over, maybe, if both of them had discussed their real feelings. But they'd been too busy trying to make the other happy.

She tore the tissues in her hands. "What if Nathan does it again?"

"Would he?" Leah arched her brows. "Or has he learned his lesson?"

"I...don't know."

Her friend patted her knee. "Seems to me you have some praying to do. Then I think you and Nathan should have a conversation about the mistakes you've made and how you'd do things differently this time." Leah paused. "Just...be careful, Cass. You've been hurt, and the instinct is to protect yourself from future pain. But there are no guarantees in life. Sometimes the people we love hurt us the most. Apologies and acts of contrition are important. But there comes a point when you have to let go and forgive."

Cassie nodded. "Thanks."

"Anytime." Leah shifted the kitten from her lap and rose, brushing off the hair from her jeans. Then she wiggled her eyebrows. "I'm gonna head into the kitchen. You've got a house of handsome, single, military men. Surely one of them will flirt with me."

LYNN SHANNON

Cassie laughed. "Watch out. Once they figure out you're single, they're going to be decking each other to get to you first."

Leah chuckled and then winked. "A girl can hope."

She left the bedroom, closing the door behind her. Cassie let the stillness settle around her. Muffin had rounded up her kittens, and they were all resting in the basket. Only the faint murmur of voices coming from the kitchen filtered into the room. Somehow, even through the walls and closed door, Cassie could still pinpoint the rumble of Nathan's voice.

The memory of their conversations, the events of the last few days, and their kiss replayed in her mind. Nathan had apologized, more than once, for his actions four years ago. His life had been threatened numerous times, and yet he stayed by her side. He'd tried countless times to gently coax her to talk to him about her feelings.

She'd refused. Cassie wasn't the reason Nathan left the first time, but she was doing a fantastic job of pushing him away now. Why? Because she was scared. But Nathan wasn't the same person he was four years ago. And neither was she.

Maybe...just maybe it was time to let go of the past. To step forward into the future.

God, that's where you're leading me, isn't it? I've been resisting you, but I'm done now. I'm sorry.

A peace stole over her, nestling in her heart. I'm sorry. Powerful words. Nathan had said them over and over, and yet Cassie had refused to forgive him. She'd been wrong. Very wrong.

Cassie rose from the carpet, determined to speak to Nathan. The timing was awful considering the threats against her, but she'd hurt him deeply yesterday and needed to apologize. And she needed to explain why she'd been so scared.

Voices grew louder as she crossed the living room. The kitchen table was full of people, including Grady and Weston. The sight of the two Texas Rangers stopped Cassie in her tracks. Every eye in the room turned in her direction. The conversation came to a halt.

Her pulse skyrocketed even as her gaze narrowed in on Nathan. "What is it?"

"Maddox Brown, the man from the flower shop, is dead." He didn't sugarcoat, knowing she wouldn't want him to. "He's been murdered."

She inhaled sharply. Cassie hadn't expected that. But she also knew there was more. "What else?"

"You were right, Cass. Holt's involved."

TWENTY-FIVE

Nathan parked in front of the veterinarian clinic and turned to face Cassie in the passenger seat. She looked stunning in a simple T-shirt that brought out the golden flecks in her eyes. Her hair was pulled back into a braid, revealing the long line of her neck and the sweet curve of her cheekbones. He wanted to toss the vehicle in reverse and drive her far, far away from here. Someplace safe. "For the record, talking to Holt yourself is a terrible idea."

She rolled her eyes. "You've said that. Like fifty million times."

"Because I'm trying to talk some sense into you."

"You can't protect me from everything, Nathan." Her voice was soft but firm. "The rangers tried to interview Holt. He refused to speak to them about Maddox, and they have no cause to arrest him. This is the best way to get answers now."

He wrestled with his conflicting emotions. Mentally, he knew Cassie was right. Each attack had been well-planned. And they were increasing in intensity. It was only by the grace of God and Cassie's bravery that Nathan survived the second encounter with the drone. Each day that passed put people at risk.

But he hated—*hated*—the idea of Cassie confronting Holt. If he was her stalker, as they believed, it would only fuel his obsession. "Kyle and I can speak to him."

"You know as well as I do Holt won't give you the time of day." She sighed. "I'm not even sure he'll speak to me now that we threw him off my property. It might be more beneficial if you wait in the truck."

"That's a no-go. This is risky enough as it is." He glared at the veterinarian clinic. "Walking in there alone could lead to all kinds of trouble. Especially if Holt feels threatened by your conversation."

Images of the man kidnapping Cassie or pulling a gun on her flashed in Nathan's mind. There was no way he would allow her to face Holt alone. It was too dangerous. The memory of the drone shooting in her direction had nearly undone him. For one moment, he'd thought Cassie had been hit. His whole world had stopped.

But she hadn't been. The incredible woman simply lifted her gun and fired back without missing a beat. She'd saved his life. And that kiss in the barn...

No, he wouldn't think about that. It was far too distracting. And distressing. Nathan had recognized the look on Cassie's face when she realized what had transpired between them. Regret, plain and simple. She hadn't forgiven him for his past mistakes and Nathan was losing hope she ever would.

He sucked in a deep breath and let it out slowly, bringing his thoughts back to the matter at hand. Confronting Holt about Maddox. "I will hang back, though, and try not to look so..."

"Protective?" A smile played on Cassie's lips. She tilted her head, her golden hair shimmering in the sunshine. "Intimidating? Fierce?"

He smiled back. Nathan had no ability to resist her. Never could. "All the above."

She chuckled. "I hate to tell you this, Nathan, but there's no chance of that happening." Her expression grew serious. "Just let me lead the conversation and we'll see where it takes us."

He nodded, reaching for the door handle. Cassie stopped him

with a hand on his arm. Her palm was silky, fingers long and femi-nine. The simple touch sent a wave of heat rushing through him, as once again, the memory of their kiss flared in his mind.

Cut it out, Hollister. Now's not the time.

He forced himself to meet her gaze. Cassie bit her lip. "When we're done, I need to talk to you about something. About us."

Fear gripped him with an iron fist that threatened to crush his lungs. She was going to tell him they were over for good. He could see it written all over her face. Nathan couldn't handle that right now. Not while her life depended on him keeping his head on straight. "Let's wait until the case is over. Once that happens, then we'll talk."

She reluctantly nodded and released his arm. Nathan exited the vehicle. He scanned the parking lot and the street beyond for any signs of danger before opening Cassie's door. Holt might be the one responsible for the attacks, but that wasn't a certainty. Jace was still out there. They didn't know how he fit into the equation yet.

The inside of the veterinarian clinic smelled like a mixture of wet dog and antiseptic. Several customers, along with their pets, sat wait-ing. Holt stood at the counter, talking with his receptionist. He caught sight of them and scowled. He quickly circled the desk to intercept them.

"What do you two want?" His voice was pitched low to keep anyone else from overhearing.

Nathan bristled at the other man's tone but schooled his expres-sion to keep the irritation from showing. They were here on a mission. He'd promised to hang back and let Cassie run the conversa-tion, and that's exactly what he intended to do. Unless...well, unless Holt became aggressive with Cassie again. Then Nathan wouldn't hesitate to step in and give the bully a taste of his own medicine.

"I need to speak to you, Holt." Cassie's tone was calm. She glanced around the waiting room. "And it would be better if we did so in private."

Holt's glower deepened, and for a moment, Nathan thought the man was going to refuse. Then he spun on his heel and, without a word, led them to an exam room. The adjustable silver table along the wall shone in the fluorescent lights. A sink was positioned in the corner, various cotton balls and pet treats stacked nearby in glass jars.

Holt closed the door behind them and crossed his arms. "I hope you're here to apologize."

Apologize? Nathan stiffened. Oh, the guy had some serious nerve. He'd practically attacked Cassie on her own front lawn for saying that she wasn't romantically interested in him. He was the one who should beg forgiveness.

Clearly, Cassie was baffled by the turn in the conversation as well. Her brow furrowed. "Come again?"

A red stain crept along Holt's neck into his cheeks. "You sent the Texas Rangers here to question me. Over nothing. A silly argument hardly needs to be a police matter, Cassie. For heaven's sake, I thought you had more sense than that."

Nathan's fingers twitched. He was sorely tempted to ball his hands into fists and finished this conversation man-to-man, but he didn't. His military training had taught him to keep control of his emotions. He tamped down his anger and forced himself to lean against the counter as if the entire conversation bored him.

"The rangers didn't come to speak to you about our argument." Cassie frowned. "They wanted to ask about Maddox Brown."

Now it was Holt's turn to look confused. "Maddox? Why on earth are the police interested in him?"

Nathan watched Holt's expression carefully. There was no indication he knew about Maddox's murder. Either Holt was a very good actor—which was possible—or he genuinely didn't know Maddox was dead.

Cassie seemed to pick up on that fact too. "The rangers believe Maddox is behind the attacks on me."

Smart woman. Holt was more likely to speak freely if he didn't believe they suspected him. Nathan kept his expression nonchalant, but his entire focus was centered on the other man.

A myriad of expressions crossed Holt's face. Surprise, then concern, and finally suspicion. "What does that have to do with me?"

"You and Maddox knew each other. Went to high school together. Several of your former neighbors said you two were quite close." Cassie lifted her brows. "I have a hard time believing Maddox was in town and never once stopped by to see you."

Holt was quiet for a long moment. He seemed to calculate his answer, trying to figure out exactly how much to tell them. That didn't bode well for his innocence.

Finally, he heaved a sigh and ran a hand over his hair. "Okay, yes, Maddox came to see me. I hadn't heard from him in over ten years, since we lost contact after high school. He showed up one day, completely out of the blue, asking for a job. I didn't have any work for him, so I sent him over to Dwayne's. I explained he often hired temporary workers for construction projects."

"When was this?"

"About a month ago." Holt held up a hand, anticipating Cassie's next questions. "No, I have no idea if he went to see Dwayne, nor did I ever see Maddox again. Honestly, I thought he'd left town."

Nathan did the math in his head. Holt and Maddox's conversation happened around the time Cassie started building her barn. There were several men they hadn't been able to identify on Dwayne's list of temporary workers.

But...Dwayne had told Chief Garcia that he didn't know the man in the composite sketch, nor did he recognize Maddox Brown when shown the prison photograph. Did Dwayne have a reason to lie? Was he involved somehow?

Was he Cassie's stalker?

TWENTY-SIX

The sound of pressure nail guns mixed with the whir of an electric saw. The barn doors had been opened wide to allow in the most sunlight. Construction workers bustled around the building, carrying wood and other supplies. A few were on the roof checking the tiles. Dwayne stood in the middle of the chaos, directing his men in the rafters to add a final layer of paneling over some installation.

Nathan studied the man. He wore a backward-facing ball cap, plaid shirt, and jeans with work boots. A pencil was stuck behind one ear. Dwayne was the general height and weight of the man who'd attacked them at the shelter, but that didn't amount to much. Half of the men in the town would fit that description.

Cassie called out Dwayne's name, drawing his attention toward her and Nathan. His face broke out into a wide smile. He ambled in their direction, waving a hand at the nearly finished barn. "What do you think?"

"It looks fantastic." She craned her head to eye the men installing the paneling above them. "You're almost finished."

"I promised to have the job complete before your fundraiser and I always make good on my promises." Dwayne planted his hands on

149

his hips. "My family is looking forward to the festivities. It's all my kids have talked about for days."

A shadow crossed Cassie's face. The fundraiser was in a few weeks, the decision to cancel it or not looming over them like a dark thundercloud. Leah had insisted they wait until later in the week, just in case there was a big break and the rangers caught the stalker. So far, that hadn't happened. Chief Garcia was still in the ICU. He'd regained consciousness for brief periods of time, but wasn't able to answer questions yet.

Based on the conversation they'd just had with Holt, Nathan was losing hope they would find the evidence necessary to narrow in on a suspect before the fundraiser deadline. But it wouldn't stop them from trying. Rescuing horses was Cassie's passion. It would break her heart if she had to cancel the event designed to launch her nonprofit.

Nathan pulled out his phone and accessed Maddox Brown's photograph. He showed it to Dwayne. "Do you know this man?"

His auburn brows drew down as he studied the picture. "No. Chief Garcia asked me about that same dude a few days ago, and I explained that I'd never seen him before." His gaze shot to Cassie. "Is this the guy that's been stalking you?"

"We're trying to figure that out. You're sure you've never seen him before? His name is Maddox Brown. It's our understanding Maddox was looking for work, and Holt sent him your way."

"Never met the guy. I'm positive about that." Dwayne frowned. "But it doesn't mean he couldn't have found work elsewhere. You're welcome to ask my crew. Maybe some of them have seen him around town and can tell you more."

Nathan didn't sense Dwayne was lying about Maddox. Had Holt sent them on a wild goose chase? If he was guilty of being Cassie's stalker, it would make sense. He'd want to muddy the case as much as possible to keep them chasing their tails while he planned his next move.

The thought made Nathan's stomach churn. They hadn't heard

from the stalker since the drone incident. He was strategizing his next move, that much was certain. They needed to find him before he could hurt anyone else.

For the next half an hour, Cassie and Nathan spoke to every member of Dwayne's crew. None of them recognized Maddox. It was frustrating and left Nathan with more questions than answers.

Kyle met them outside near the fence line. His cousin had lost any interest in hiding the fact that he was armed. His holster was clearly visible on his belt, his handgun resting inside. He'd been patrolling the property for most of the morning. Jason would take over in the afternoon.

"What did y'all find out?" Kyle asked, adjusting his cowboy hat against the blinding sun.

"Nothing very helpful." Nathan gave him a quick overview of the conversations. "None of this makes sense. We're missing something."

"What do you mean?" Cassie asked.

She lifted her hand to shield her eyes in order to see him better. Nathan took off his ball cap and plopped it on her head. It was several sizes too big for her. She looked adorable in it though.

"Well, for starters, how does Jace fit into all of this?" Nathan couldn't get that nagging thought out of his head. "We haven't been able to connect him to either Maddox or Holt. The fact that he was outside the hospital leads me to believe someone told him to be there."

"Or he could be the stalker and we've been chasing rabbit trails designed to mislead us this whole time," Kyle pointed out. "Just because we haven't found a connection between Jace and Maddox doesn't mean there isn't one. They could've known each other casually. Gone to the same bar or had a friend in common. Logan is still wading through every one of Jace's friends on his social media. He has tons."

Nathan nodded. "I suppose. I just find it hard to believe that if

Jace was the stalker, that he'd hire someone he didn't know well to send Cassie roses."

"Maddox was interested in money. Nothing else. I'm sorry to speak ill of the dead, but he'd turn on his own mother if it would put a dollar in his pocket. Maddox is exactly the type of person someone like Jace would hire to do his dirty work."

"Do we know anything more about his murder?" Cassie asked.

"Nothing more than we did yesterday."

Maddox had been shot coming out of his apartment in the dead of night. There were no witnesses and no signs of a struggle. Whoever had killed him had been quick and effective. Or had used a drone. Which seemed likely given the number of times they'd been attacked in the same way.

Nathan rocked back on his heels. "Well, we can connect Holt and Maddox. Trouble with that is, Holt didn't act as if he knew Maddox was dead. He could've been faking it, but his reaction seemed genuine." He scrubbed a hand over his face. There were too many possibilities, too many unknowns. "Like I said, nothing about this makes sense."

Cassie's phone beeped with an incoming message. She pulled it from her pocket and glanced at the screen. Her complexion instantly paled and her knee buckled. Nathan caught her before she collapsed on the ground. He hugged her close, but Cassie's gaze never left the phone screen. Tears ran down her face. Desperation made Nathan try to take the phone from her hands, but she wouldn't release it.

"Cassie, let me see."

"It's Eric." Her voice came out on a wail. "He's been kidnapped."

TWENTY-SEVEN

Twenty minutes later, Cassie was still staring at the photograph on her phone. Eric was curled up in a ball inside what looked to be the trunk of a car. His mouth was taped shut, his feet and hands bound. Tear tracks streaked down his cheeks. Even though he wasn't looking straight at the camera, Eric's terror was evident.

Underneath the picture was one line of text.

I have something important to you.

Nathan and Kyle's voices spilled out of the kitchen. Their words were indistinguishable as they spoke to the Texas Rangers. Papa Joe sat on the couch beside her, holding his Bible and praying. The gentle lilt of his voice and the words he spoke aloud were the only balm to Cassie's pain. Her heart was breaking in two, and she trusted God knew that without her saying it out loud. The only thought Cassie could form repeated in a round robin in her head.

Please keep Eric safe until we can find him.

It was tempting to slip back into her old routine, to believe that God had abandoned Eric and her. But it wasn't true. Her conversation with Leah had forever changed Cassie's viewpoint. She had to look through a different lens. This was an opportunity to lean on

God, not turn away from Him. He was a source of strength. One she desperately needed at this moment.

Through the thick haze of her grief, Cassie heard Nathan say Tucker's name. She bolted from the couch and went into the kitchen. Nathan and Kyle surrounded a cell phone propped up on the counter.

Cassie joined them and nearly gasped. Tucker's bruised and battered face filled the screen. Blood was matted in his hair and a horrific gash on his forehead still oozed. His lip was split open in two places. She could hardly believe he was conscious given the enlarged goose egg forming near his right temple. Someone's hands—a nurse's or a doctor's—came into view. Tucker waved them away, ordering them to back off before he got up and walked out of the hospital.

Nathan pulled Cassie closer. "Calm down, Tucker, before they give you a sedative."

A few more terse words were exchanged with someone off-screen. Tucker seemed to have won the battle with the staff because he focused back on the phone. "We were ambushed. Two guys driving a four-door sedan. Black or dark blue, with Texas plates, first three letters are Tango-Kappa-Bravo."

Kyle scribbled down every word. "T-K-B. Got it. Make or model on the car?"

"American, I know that much. Ford or Dodge." Tucker winced. "I screwed up, guys. I didn't see them coming. Eric and I were riding bicycles together. He was ahead of me, crossing the street with his bike, when they rounded the corner and took me down."

Cassie inhaled sharply. "They ran over you with the car?"

"They didn't so much run over me as flip me onto the hood and then back up real fast, so I slid off into the street. One minute Eric was in front of me, the next I was groaning on the asphalt." Tucker blinked fast as if he was attempting to hold back tears. "Eric ran straight for me. He wanted to help me. I tried to tell him to run but..."

Cassie felt her own tears welling up to flood her vision. Of course,

Eric had tried to help. It's who he was. Kind, gentle, sweet. Thinking about him in the clutches of her stalker sent powerful waves of anger through her followed by paralyzing fear.

Nathan wrapped an arm around her waist, drawing her against his side, as if he sensed her fraying emotions. Probably did. She leaned into his touch. He loved Eric, too, and this had to be killing him almost as much as it was her.

Tucker swallowed hard. "The men grabbed Eric. It all happened so fast and my head was spinning. I didn't even get a good look at them. Only the license plate as they drove away."

It was a miracle he'd gotten that given the shape he was in. It was obvious Tucker was blaming himself for what happened. But it wasn't his fault. Her thoughts were confirmed when Tucker said, "I'm sorry, Cassie—"

"Don't apologize." She leaned closer to the phone so he could clearly see her face. He needed to realize she wasn't speaking these words lightly. "You have nothing to be sorry for. This isn't your fault, Tucker. We'll find him."

He nodded, but the worry in his eyes didn't dissipate. Nathan and Kyle asked a few more questions about the assault, but Tucker couldn't remember any more. They hung up so he could get the medical care he needed.

"I'll call Grady and Weston," Kyle said. "They're heading up the investigation and they'll want to know what Tucker said. I'll also do a patrol of the property."

He opened the back door, letting in fragrant spring air. Cassie watched Kyle cross the yard, phone to his ear, and an idea formed in her mind. She turned it over, examining all sides. There was no other option. Even if the Texas Rangers worked day and night, it might take them days to figure out where Eric was.

She didn't think Eric had days.

Cassie chewed on her bottom lip. "We need to strategize."

Nathan straightened his spine. "What do you mean?"

He wouldn't like what she was going to say next. But the last hour had been the worst of her life. She couldn't—wouldn't—risk Eric's life. He was like a little brother to her. He was family. And she was the reason he was in trouble. Every threat, since this whole thing began, centered around one thing: her.

Cassie wrapped her arms around herself. "You and Kyle need to go. Papa Joe too. The stalker wants an opportunity to get me. We need to give it to him."

"What?" Nathan's eyes widened. "Absolutely not."

"It's the only way to save Eric."

"I'm not leaving you here unprotected."

"I won't be unprotected." She pointed to Bruiser, standing guard nearby. The dog had been following her around since she entered the house. He seemed to have sensed her distress and was attempting to provide comfort. "I also have my gun and I know how to shoot."

"Cassie, that's a horrible idea." He crossed the room and gripped her arms, probably more tightly than he intended. A panic she'd never seen in the calm-under-fire Nathan lined every muscle in his body. "This guy isn't looking to simply kill you. He wants to keep you, possess you. He's obsessed. He'll—"

Nathan cut off as if he'd choked on the word. Cassie placed a palm over his heart. It was beating a mile a minute. "I know the risks and I'm willing to accept them. It's my choice."

His mouth opened as if to argue and then slammed shut. Nathan knew as well as she did that it was her decision. He didn't approve. Not one bit. But Cassie had never expected him to.

Nathan sucked in a breath and then let it out slowly. "Okay, Cass. You want to lure the stalker here. We can do that." He met her gaze. "But I'd like you to hear me out. There may be a way to do it so we can both get what we want."

She was determined, but she wasn't reckless. Cassie nodded. "I'm listening."

TWENTY-EIGHT

Nearly midnight and still nothing.

Nathan lifted his night-vision goggles and scanned the broad expanse of lawn in front of the Cassie's house. Nothing. He swept across the forest near the barn, catching sight of a fox, but not the stalker. An owl hooted overhead.

What was he waiting for? Nathan, Kyle, and Papa Joe had made a big show of leaving the house hours ago. But not before taking precautions. Cassie was wearing a tracker and a microphone. Nathan could hear her talking to Bruiser in a low voice. Spoiling the dog again. It brought a smile to his face.

"You're awfully happy to be on a stakeout," Kyle kept his voice pitched low. "Especially considering the love of your life is being used as bait."

"She's talking to Bruiser." Nathan lowered his night-vision goggles. "Trust me. I'm not thrilled about using Cassie as bait, but she's one of the most stubborn people I've ever met. Once she makes up her mind about something, there's no convincing her otherwise."

Kyle shooed away a mosquito. "Where do things stand with you guys these days?"

"I have no idea." Nathan sighed. "I've apologized, I've told her what I want, but...I hurt her, Kyle. Deeply. I don't know if she can ever forgive me."

His cousin was quiet. Kyle knew better than anyone the pain Nathan had put Cassie through. He'd been the one to deliver the breakup note four years ago. He'd also desperately tried to talk Nathan out of making a rash decision. One he would regret.

"I gave up on her," Nathan continued. "On us. It was easy for me to say that Cassie would refuse to listen, that it was better to make a clean break of things, but that's not the truth. At least, not all of it."

"Care to share the missing piece?"

Nathan adjusted his stance. He'd never told this part to anyone before, never spoken the words out loud. "I was scared. I made a promise to my mom. The last time I saw her in the hospital, she made me swear to follow my dreams. To become a Green Beret."

He could still remember the harsh smell of bleach, the beeping of the machines, the feel of his mom's delicate and fragile hand. A world of worry had been in her eyes. Not for herself. For him. They'd been a team since the moment he was born. Losing her had crushed him. There were days that promise he made to her was the only reason he got out of bed in the morning.

"I was determined to make Mom proud," Nathan continued. "And everything was on track until I met Cassie. I fell in love with her, but the more I learned about her past, the more I worried my career would break us. I didn't think it was possible to provide her with the security she needed. That she deserved."

And for the thousandth time, Nathan beat himself up for hiding what was going on from her. Could he have saved his relationship with Cassie if he'd made different choices? Explained what was going on inside his head? He'd never know.

"Cassie is so much stronger than I gave her credit for, Kyle." These last few days proved that. Shame filled Nathan. "I should've fought harder for us. Sat her down and told her what was going on, how I was feeling. I was a coward."

Kyle was quiet for a long moment. "You lost your way, Nathan. It happens to all of us. The thing is to learn from your mistakes, to apologize, and then...let it go. You've done all you can to prove to Cassie how sorry you are. Whether she forgives you or not, you need to forgive yourself."

That was a tall order, but Nathan knew in his heart that his cousin was right. He'd regret his choice to leave Cassie four years ago for the rest of his life, but he couldn't allow one terrible decision to define him.

It also couldn't define his relationship with Cassie forever. At the end of the day, the decision about where they went from here was hers. Either she would fully forgive him or she wouldn't. Nathan hoped it was the former, but if it was the latter, then he would accept it and, finally, move on.

Was that why God had brought him back into Cassie's life? Maybe their relationship wasn't meant to be mended. Maybe Nathan was here to save her from a killer and heal himself.

A ringing phone vibrated in Nathan's earpiece, interrupting the train of his thoughts. He stiffened. The stalker was calling. Nathan gestured to Kyle to let him know it was showtime. His cousin immediately started scanning the yard again.

Cassie answered the call. "I got your message and sent Nathan and the others away. I want to speak to Eric."

"And you will, sugar plum. Drive to the coordinates I'm sending to your phone. And don't try to trick me. If I see anyone, and I mean anyone, following you, then I'll kill Eric."

He hung up before she could say another word.

Nathan's jaw clenched, and he shot a look at his cousin. "The stalker knows we're here. He just ordered Cassie to drive to another location."

"He knows you'd never leave her vulnerable. I didn't think this plan would work in the first place. But we had to try."

Nathan's phone rang. Cassie. He answered it. "I heard."

"He sent me the coordinates. It's some kind of cabin about fifteen minutes away." She swallowed hard. "I have to go, Nathan. If I don't, he'll simply kill Eric to punish me."

"I know." He weighed his options. There was a small possibility that Eric was already dead, but Nathan didn't think so. The stalker kidnapped him to lure Cassie onto his turf. He also wanted to hurt her, and what better way to do that than to kill Eric right in front of her.

There wasn't enough time to do reconnaissance on the new location. It complicated his ability to keep her safe, exactly what the killer was counting on. "Send me the coordinates, Cass. I'll tell the other guys to hang back and wait for my word. Do you remember everything I told you?"

They'd planned for numerous contingencies. Including this one. Nathan hated, *hated*, the idea of putting Cassie at risk, but she wouldn't be talked out of it. Not with Eric's life hanging in the balance.

"I remember everything we discussed." She was quiet for a beat. "If he sees you..."

"I'm a Green Beret, Cass. He won't know I'm there." Nathan had the urge to say how much he loved her but swallowed the temptation down. Cassie was already going through more than any person should. He wouldn't add to that by speaking his feelings out loud when it would only add to her bucket of problems. "You won't know I'm there either, but I will be. Trust me."

He hung up. Logan, Jason, and Walker were stationed at different locations on the property. "Radio the guys and tell them not to follow Cassie or me. I'll send you the coordinates. Give us a ten-minute head start. And do your best to figure out who owns that cabin before Cassie gets there."

Kyle grabbed his arm. Even in the dim moonlight, concern reflected in his expression. "Nathan, the stalker is counting on you to go after Cassie. He wants to kill you as much as he wants to possess her."

"I know."

TWENTY-NINE

Cassie gripped the steering wheel of the rental vehicle so tightly her hands hurt. Her truck was still in the repair shop after the first drone shootout. The GPS calculated she was ten minutes from her destination. It was reckless to be meeting a killer, but what other option did she have? Eric's life was on the line, and she would gladly sacrifice herself to save her surrogate little brother.

She prayed it wouldn't come to that.

Tall trees lined both sides of the country road, blocking out most of the moonlight. Her headlights sliced through the darkness. Cassie hadn't passed another vehicle since leaving her ranch. She glanced in the rearview mirror, but there wasn't a car behind her. Still, she knew Nathan was there. If she couldn't spot him, hopefully that meant her stalker wouldn't either.

Please, God. I need you more than ever. Give me the wisdom to make the right decisions and the strength to follow them. And please watch over Nathan and Eric.

The GPS directed Cassie to turn onto a small dirt road. She did. Fear crept up her spine, stealing her breath as the darkness pressed in closer. Her wheels rolled over dips and ruts. Overgrown bushes scraped the sides of her sedan, creating a high-pitched sound that frayed her nerves. Her heart beat faster. Cassie's survival instinct was screaming at her to turn the car around and flee. It was only her love for Eric that kept her moving forward.

A cabin came into view. At any other time, Cassie would've found it cute and rustic. Stone and wood blended together in seamless architecture. Neat flower beds contained a wide display of wildflowers and the porch held two rocking chairs alongside a moveable fire pit.

According to the map, Cassie was upstream from her own property. The river was hidden behind a wall of trees, but the rushing current was loud enough to hear, even through the closed windows of her sedan.

She shut off her vehicle. The ticking sound of the engine cooling felt like a time bomb. Cassie wasn't trained for this. She wasn't a police officer. She hadn't even taken a self-defense class. But she was a survivor. Abuse, neglect, abandonment. Nothing had broken her. Cassie wouldn't allow it to. She would need every ounce of that grit and determination to get her through this.

Cassie exited the car. The night air was chilly against her overheated skin. She pulled her handgun, flipping off the safety. Her gaze tracked across the woods and the cabin. Nothing moved.

Was Eric inside? Or had the stalker lured her here to kidnap her? There was no way to know. Cassie had removed the microphone—it would be visible upon close inspection—but the tracker was still in her shoe. If she was taken, Nathan would be able to find her location.

Sucking in a deep breath, she tamped down her fear. Dried leaves crunched under her feet. The windows of the cabin were shut tight, blinds drawn, making it impossible to see inside. Cicadas chirped. Cassie kept her ears pricked for any unusual sound, but nothing stirred.

She reached the cabin door. The porch light didn't flick on. Cassie flexed the fingers holding her weapon and then wrapped them back around the grip. The door handle was cold under her palm. She spared one last glance over her shoulder and then twisted the knob.

The door creaked open.

The interior of the cabin was pitch-black. Cassie entered, leading with her weapon, spinning quickly to check behind the door.

No one was there.

He was playing with her. She could feel it. Someone was in the house, watching, waiting. Goose bumps skittered across her skin. Her breathing increased, and it took physical effort to slow it down before she hyperventilated.

Cassie left the front door open, letting the moonlight guide her way. Her eyes adjusted to the dark. A cozy living room flowed into a tiny kitchen. A dark hallway shot off to the left. The sour taste of fear filled her mouth. She swallowed it back down, forcing herself to take one step. Then another.

Eric could be in the house. In a back bedroom. He could be hurt, possibly bleeding out. This could be simply another trick by her stalker to teach her a "lesson" like he'd done with Chief Garcia.

Pulse pounding, Cassie reached the hall. Darkened rooms shot off from either side. It was like something from a horror movie. Her hand tightened on her weapon, and she kept her senses alert for any sound or movement. Thick carpeting sank under her feet.

The first bedroom and en suite bathroom were empty. The second as well. Cassie reached the last bedroom in the hallway.

A canopy bed was flanked by two nightstands. The bathroom door was tilted open, providing a partial view of the interior. Cassie stepped inside, reaching for the closed shower curtain to check the tub.

Air shifted behind her. She spun, but not fast enough. Her attacker flew out from behind the partially closed door and slammed into her with the force of a linebacker. Cassie flew into the wall. Her forehead rammed against the faucet as she tumbled into the tub and pain shot through her. Somehow, she held on to her weapon.

She whirled, liquid flooding her vision, blinding her. Blood. Cassie fired, but the bullet missed its target. The attacker—dressed in all black and a ski mask—grabbed her arm. He slammed her hand against the edge of the bathtub with enough force to break her fingers. She screamed as the appendage went numb. The gun dropped to the floor.

A gloved hand gripped her throat, turning her face to the side. Just as he'd done in the first assault, he leaned down and smelled her neck. His breath was hot and vulgar. Bile burned her throat. She swallowed it back down, gritting her teeth. "Where's Eric?"

"All in good time, sugar plum." He pulled back. In the darkness, his eyes were nothing but black holes. "You tried to shoot me."

She didn't recognize his voice at all. He had a thick Texas drawl. "You expected it."

"I did. Identifying me would enable you to find your precious Eric." He chuckled as if they were flirting or playing some kind of sick game. "I'm going to tie you up now. If you want Eric to stay alive, I suggest you comply. Otherwise, it'll be unpleasant for everyone."

Cassie let her muscles go lax. Plan A had failed. It was time to shift to Plan B. Eric wasn't in the house. She knew that for sure. "Where is he?"

"You'll see."

Clamping an iron grip around her wrists, he hauled her from the bathtub and secured her arms behind her back with flex cuffs. The plastic cut into her skin. Blood from the gash on her forehead was still dripping into her eyes. She swiped her face against her shoulder, attempting to clear her vision using her shirt. It took everything inside her not to resist when the killer shoved a rag into her mouth and slapped tape over her lips.

Nathan was out there. They'd known this was a possibility, had discussed it during their strategy session. Cassie had to keep it together long enough for him to make a plan to capture her stalker.

To save Eric. They were going to end this, one way or another, tonight.

"Walk, sugar plum."

The barrel of a gun pressed against her back. Cassie's legs trembled, but somehow she did as instructed. He led her to the kitchen pantry and then opened the door. Light blinded her as the bulb overhead automatically came on. She blinked, forcing her eyes to adjust.

"Keep going."

There was another door, already open inside. A concrete pathway extended downward. Cassie couldn't make heads or tails of it until they were inside the structure. It was an underground tunnel. The sound of the river grew louder and then suddenly they were outside.

A scream broke through the night air. The killer grabbed Cassie around the waist, holding her tight against him. She gave into her instincts and struggled against him, but it was no use. He merely tightened his hold.

Her heart thundered against her chest. Another scream echoed. Belatedly, Cassie realized it was her voice. But it was coming from inside the cabin.

"A little recording I made from our first interaction," he whispered in her ear. "I made it for myself, but it's going to come in handy now."

Cassie's skin crawled at his nearness. It was hard to process his words. What was he talking about?

He took out a cell phone and flipped to some kind of app. Cassie's breaths were shallow, his arm like a vise around her, and then she caught sight of a dark shape racing toward the cabin. Her gut clenched as her mind instantly recognized the man she loved.

Nathan.

No! Her brain screamed the word, even though her mouth couldn't utter it past the gag. She fought and struggled against the killer's hold like a wild cat, but it was no use. Another scream came from inside the cabin, followed by gunshots. Nathan disappeared around the side and a bang came, as though he'd kicked down the front door.

Time seemed to slow down as Cassie's gaze dropped to her attacker's gloved finger. Horror filled her as he pressed a button on his cell phone.

The cabin exploded.

THIRTY

Tears dripped down Cassie's face, dropping onto the metal bottom of the dingy carrying her to God knew where. Her kidnapper was humming as he steered the boat, powered by a small motor, down the river. He still wore the ski mask over his face. Nothing about him was familiar, or maybe her brain refused to fully process what was happening.

Nathan was dead.

The thought brought a swell of fresh tears Cassie couldn't hold back. A sob threatened to steal what little breath she could drag into her lungs through her nose, since the gag still filled her mouth. The time she'd spent with Nathan flashed through her mind in rapid succession like Cassie's own personal movie. From the moment he stepped out of the truck in North Carolina to help her with a flat, to their first kiss, to their last conversation. Every touch, every glance, every precious moment...

All the pain and anger she'd been holding on to over his mistake paled in comparison to the joy he'd brought to her life. Cassie's heart splintered in two. She'd forgiven Nathan, planned to tell him she was in love with him, but they'd never had that conversation. And now they never would.

It was, by far, the darkest moment of her life. The pain was so engrossing it was physical in its intensity. Her whole body trembled.

God, why? Why?

The boat knocked against a wooden dock, jolting Cassie from her thoughts. She drew in a breath, then another, willing her body to calm down. She couldn't give up. Couldn't shut down. Eric needed her. She had to stay strong for him.

He was alive. Cassie knew that much. Her stalker had kidnapped him intending to kill Eric in front of her. That was the kind of man he was. She wouldn't let it happen. The tracker was still in her shoe, providing Kyle and the rest of Nathan's friends with her location. They would come after her. Cassie didn't doubt that either.

Nathan had promised they would.

The boat rocked as the stalker tied to the dock. Then he hauled Cassie up, tossing her over his shoulder as if she were a sack of potatoes, and started walking. She craned her head, attempting to get a look at her surroundings. Grass, trees, and the river. Nothing familiar. The wound on her forehead began bleeding again. She had a pounding headache that made her nauseous. Or maybe that was the fear churning her stomach.

They entered a house, but Cassie only saw a tile floor before she was carried down a set of stairs. Her kidnapper tossed her onto an old, torn couch. She landed on her swollen, broken hand. Cassie's cry was muffled by the gag.

"Sorry, sugar plum." He ripped the tape off her mouth, nearly taking a layer of skin with it.

Cassie spat out the rag in her mouth. Her mouth felt like cotton. Her gaze jumped around the room. They were in a basement. Tool boxes lined one wall, but it was the man tied to the chair that snagged her attention. Eric! He was alive but unconscious, his chin resting on his chest. She couldn't see him well, but he appeared unharmed.

For now.

Cassie scrambled to sit up on the couch, ignoring the screaming pain coming from her right hand. It was definitely broken. She eyed the man standing in front of her. He was still wearing the ski mask.

"I told you, sugar plum." He lifted his hands, tucking his thumbs underneath the bottom of the mask and lifting it. "Eric's just fine."

Cassie gasped. Her mouth dropped open, but no words would form on her lips.

Dwayne Booth, her contractor.

He smirked, his expression dark and twisted. "Surprise."

"You..." She couldn't form a coherent thought. Dwayne had never been on her radar as a suspect. Cassie swallowed hard, trying to make sense of things. "I don't understand."

He reached out a hand to touch her hair. Cassie jerked away. Dwayne ignored her reaction, grabbing a fistful of strands and tugging her closer to him. He trailed a finger down her cheek and along her jaw. "What is there to understand? You and I are meant to be. I knew it from the first moment I saw you."

Oh, she was going to be sick. "But...you're married."

"She left me. A few months ago, but no one knows that. I've told everyone that she's taking care of a sick relative. It doesn't matter. My wife means nothing to me and never has. It's always been you, sugar plum."

He was delusional. Absolutely delusional. How had Cassie never noticed? He'd kept it so well hidden. No one knew. Trembles racked her body, despite her best attempts to quell them. His nasty hand brushed against her throat, pausing right above the pulse point. Her heart was racing. Cassie knew he could feel it from the way his eyes widened. A twisty pleasure sparked across his expression. He liked her fear.

God, help me.

"I'm sure you're wondering about my accent. My mother forced me to take speech lessons, but this Texas twang is my real voice. Do you love it?"

Cassie couldn't stand it, but something inside her said she should agree with him. She nodded.

Dwayne smiled, as if her answer pleased him. "I knew when you moved back to town, it was time for us to have our chance." He paused. The grin slowly melted from his face. "But you wouldn't give me the time of day."

Panic filled Cassie as his expression turned dark and twisted. Evil. She tried to pull away, but he only tightened his grip on her hair. Strands ripped from her scalp as he twisted her neck so hard, Cassie feared it would snap.

Dwayne glared at her. "You only had eyes for Nathan."

He reared back and smacked her. Pain exploded along her cheekbone. Cassie cried out, falling back against the couch. She stared at Dwayne through tear-filled eyes as he patted the cheek he'd just hit. His expression was sorrowful. "I'm sorry, but I can't let things like that go unpunished. That's why Nathan had to die."

The switch in his emotions was terrifying. Cassie couldn't stop the chills from shaking her. She desperately tried to break free of the plastic cuffs, but every move of her hand sent agony arching through her. Tears pricked her eyes, but she swallowed them back. She wouldn't give him the satisfaction of seeing her cry.

Dwayne pulled out a gun from under his shirt. "I need you to understand, Cassie. There's no one in the world except me." He cast a derisive look in Eric's direction, pointing the gun at the unconscious man. "I'm the only one who loves you."

He was going to shoot Eric. Desperation had her tugging harder at the binds, but they refused to budge. "Wait, please, wait. There's nothing romantic between Eric and I. We're like siblings. There's no need to kill him." She sucked in a breath so sharp it made her lungs ache. "Let him go and I'll do whatever you want."

Dwayne tilted his head, as if pondering her statement. Cassie gave up on trying to undo the cuffs and tilted forward on the couch. Where were Kyle and the others? She and Eric were running out of time.

Cassie met her captor's gaze. "I promise. I'll do whatever you want, Dwayne. Let Eric go and you'll have my complete loyalty."

Dwayne ambled over to her, a smile quirking the corners of his mouth. He leaned down close, as if he was going to kiss her cheek. Cassie stilled. Her heart thundered against her rib cage.

"Sugar plum, there's something you need to understand right now. Your loyalty is already mine."

He whirled, pointing the gun at Eric. Cassie screamed. She threw herself off the couch and slammed into Dwayne. They tumbled to the concrete floor in a mass of arms and legs. The gun went off. Pain, fierce and sharp, iced through Cassie's upper arm. Black spots danced across her vision.

Dwayne stood up, his hair mussed, his expression deadly cold. "You're going to pay for that."

He picked up the gun again. Cassie tried to move, but it was like fighting against quicksand. Her body wouldn't respond to her brain's commands fast enough. Dwayne pointed the gun at Eric once more.

A bang resounded through the room, bouncing off the concrete space. Smoke filled the space. Tears instantly flooded Cassie's vision as coughs overtook her. Feet pounded on the stairs, followed by Dwayne's scream. Panic overtook Cassie as she tried to force her body to move, to find Eric. Was he okay? Had he been shot?

A man wearing a gas mask appeared in front of her. Gentle hands lifted her from the ground and then she was moving up the stairs and out of the house. Her savior sat her down on the grass. Cool water washed the burning irritant from her eyes. Cassie blinked, struggling to clear her vision.

Her heart stopped as familiar brilliant green eyes came into focus. She shook her head, unable to comprehend what she was seeing. No, it couldn't be. Cassie touched his face, the bristles on his cheek pricking her palm. "Nathan..."

He was alive. Words clogged her throat, cutting off any possibility of speech.

Nathan kissed her on the lips. It was tender and sweet, and not nearly long enough. Then he backed away to remove his shirt. "Cass, you've been shot."

She couldn't feel a thing. She looked down and was shocked to discover blood running down her arm. Nathan tore his shirt into strips and wrapped them around the wound. "We have to get you to a hospital."

Shot. Eric. Cassie struggled against Nathan's ministrations. "Eric! Where is he? Is he okay?"

"He's fine, Cass." Nathan pushed her back down to the grass and pointed a short distance away. Eric was being tended to by Kyle. Nathan's cousin must've heard Cassie's questions because he glanced in their direction.

"Pulse is strong, and he's breathing fine. No sign of any injuries, other than a few bruises. He's probably been drugged. A couple of ambulances are already on the way, along with the Texas Rangers." Kyle cocked a smile. "You did good, Cassie."

Relief washed over her in a flood. "Thank you, God. Thank you."

"You can say that again." Nathan cupped her face. "We've got Dwayne secured. He won't see the outside of a prison cell ever again. It's over, Cass. It's all over."

Sirens wailed in the distance. In a few minutes, the area would be flooded with more people. Cassie hadn't said what she'd wanted to earlier, and nothing was going to keep her from doing it now. "I love you, Nathan. I love you with everything inside me."

He inhaled sharply. Hope flared in his eyes. "Cass—"

"Let me say this, please. What happened between us four years ago was painful, but it doesn't erase all the love between us. We have a second chance at happiness. I want to take it."

Nathan swept his thumb over the curve of her cheek. His gaze lifted to the cut on her head before meeting hers. His mouth quirked. "Do you really mean that or is it the concussion talking?"

She brushed her mouth against his in reply. The kiss started out tender, but passion took over until they were both breathless. Cassie pulled back to look in his eyes. The love shining there bathed her in warmth. "I'm sorry it took me so long to find my way to forgiveness."

"Don't apologize. All that matters is that we're together now. I love you, Cass."

"I love you too."

THIRTY-ONE

One month later

Nathan clutched Cassie's hand as they hurried down the church steps. His new cowboy boots—bought to go with his tux—didn't have the best tread for sprinting away from overeager guests armed with birdseed. He doubted his bride's shoes were up to the task either. Although she could be wearing tennis shoes under that gorgeous wedding dress, and he wouldn't know it.

Cassie laughed, her beautiful face lighting up with joy as she was showered with enough food to keep the birds eating for a week. Nathan couldn't help laughing with her. Their guests shouted and cheered as Nathan held open the door of his truck for his bride. He helped her in, tucked yards of fabric around her, and then shut the door.

Kyle blasted him in the face with a mountain of bird seed. Nathan shoved his cousin and then dodged the other four handfuls coming in his direction. He glared at his friends on the church stairs.

"Keep that up and I'll deny your admission to the reception. There's steak. And cake."

His buddies wisely decided to pelt each other with the birdseed. Nathan chuckled as he got into the truck. Cassie grinned, leaning over to kiss him. "Hello, husband."

Husband. He loved the sound of that. He cupped her face and deepened the kiss. Nathan was so lost in her, it took a few moments to realize there was wild cheering coming from the crowd outside. He broke off the kiss, resting his forehead against hers. "Can we skip the reception?"

She laughed and playfully swatted at him. "No. Papa Joe would be heartbroken if we did. He's been planning the whole event for weeks with Leah. Just a word of warning. I think she's putting bows on all the animals."

"All?" Nathan arched his brows, firing up the engine of his truck. "Including Bruiser? And Starlight?"

Cassie nodded. "Even Muffin. She's going all out."

Nathan groaned, but it was all in teasing fun. In the last few weeks, he'd grown close to Cassie's best friend. She'd been a tremendous help in planning the wedding. The short time span had proven challenging, but neither Nathan nor Cassie had wanted to wait to start their life together. Leah's help had made their dream possible.

Not that Nathan cared about the tux or the dinner. But Cassie's grandfather did. Papa Joe was a romantic at heart and he wanted to marry his only grandchild off in style. Nathan was happy to go along with anything, as long as he got to call Cassie his wife.

His wife. He loved the sound of that.

Nathan reached for Cassie's hand, but she was rubbing her arm. Her injured arm. Concern shot through him. "What's the matter? Are you okay?"

"I'm fine. It's just a bit sore." She dropped her hand, a smile curving her lips. "You know what occurred to me the other day? Now you and I have matching bullet wounds."

"That's not funny." He snagged her hand, lifting it to his lips. Nathan didn't like to think about how close he'd come to losing her.

Dwayne had refused to talk to the police, but the Texas Rangers figured out most of what happened. The thugs that kidnapped Eric were arrested. They'd worked for Dwayne briefly, and then kept in touch. When he called to offer them money—a lot of money—to kill Tucker and kidnap Eric, they jumped at it.

Maddox Brown had probably done the same. Instead of giving the man construction work, Dwayne hired him to send Cassie roses. Then killed him once Maddox was connected to the case.

Dwayne had worked on Cassie's property for months. He'd learned the layout and become familiar with the horses. Starlight had known and trusted him. Even the drone made sense. Dwayne's wife was a professional photographer and used them for her work.

The evidence piled up, and once he faced the potential of the death penalty, Dwayne agreed to life in prison without the possibility of parole. He would never hurt anyone ever again, including Cassie.

Nathan was very grateful for that.

He kissed Cassie's hand again. "No more tangling with bullets, okay? I need you for at least the next seventy years or so."

A wistful look came over her face. "Do you think we'll be that couple sitting on the porch with our grandkids and great-grandkids scattered about?"

It was a wonderful image. Nathan tossed her a smile. "I'm planning on it, sweetheart."

He turned onto the road leading to the ranch. Tents were set up on the lawn, twinkling lights covering everything standing still. Cassie gasped. "Oh, it's so beautiful."

It was. Nathan spotted Bessie and Eric standing together, arms wrapped around one another. Leah came out of the house along with Papa Joe. All of them had left the wedding right after the ceremony to help set up for the reception.

Bruiser spotted the truck and came running. Sure enough, he was wearing a blue bow around his neck. Spoiled dog. His spoiled dog, to be exact. Nathan had permanently adopted him weeks ago.

He got out of the truck, pointing a finger at his pit bull. "No jumping. I'm wearing a tux."

The dog's butt hit the ground, and he wagged his tail. Nathan patted his head before circling the vehicle to help Cassie out. She slipped her hand into his, and a jolt of electricity raced up his arm. He leaned in to kiss her lips softly. The woman undid him.

"Just so you know, I meant what I said." Nathan brushed her mouth with his lips again. "I promised that if you gave me a second chance, I'd spent the rest of my life proving to you it wasn't a mistake. I'm going to make you the happiest woman on earth."

She wrapped her arms around him. "You already do."

ALSO BY LYNN SHANNON

Texas Ranger Heroes Series

Ranger Protection

Ranger Redemption

Ranger Courage

Ranger Faith

Ranger Honor

Triumph Over Adversity Series

Calculated Risk

Critical Error

Necessary Peril

Would you like to know when my next book is released? Or when my novels go on sale? It's easy. Subscribe to my newsletter at www. lynnshannon.com and all of the info will come straight to your inbox!

Reviews help readers find books. Please consider leaving a review at your favorite place of purchase or anywhere you discover new books. Thank you.